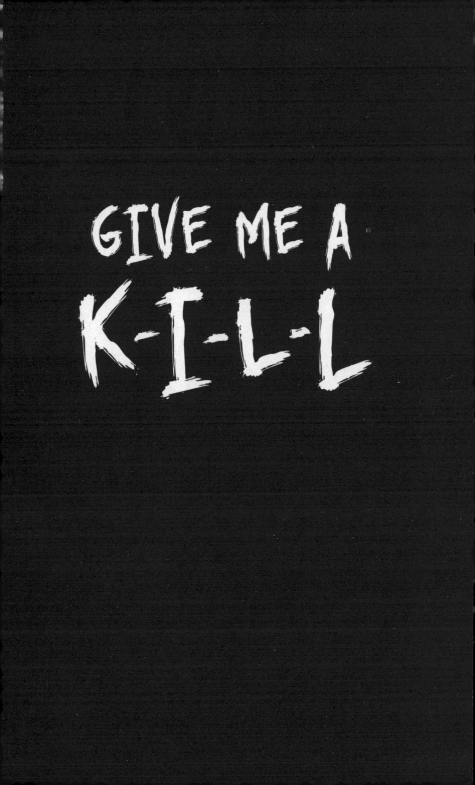

R. L. STINE

GIVE ME A
K-I-L-L

A *FEAR STREET* NOVEL

THOMAS DUNNE BOOKS
ST. MARTIN'S GRIFFIN
NEW YORK

THOMAS DUNNE BOOKS.
An imprint of St. Martin's Press.

GIVE ME A K-I-L-L. Copyright © 2017 by Parachute Publishing, L.L.C. All rights reserved. Printed in the United States of America. For information, address St. Martin's Press, 175 Fifth Avenue, New York, N.Y. 10010.

www.thomasdunnebooks.com
www.stmartins.com

The Library of Congress Cataloging-in-Publication Data is available upon request.

ISBN 978-1-250-05896-6 (hardcover)
ISBN 978-1-250-14352-5 (International, sold outside the U.S., subject to rights availability)
ISBN 978-1-250-11698-7 (e-book)

Our books may be purchased in bulk for promotional, educational, or business use. Please contact your local bookseller or the Macmillan Corporate and Premium Sales Department at 1-800-221-7945, extension 5442, or by e-mail at MacmillanSpecialMarkets@macmillan.com.

First U.S. Edition: April 2017
First International Edition: April 2017

10 9 8 7 6 5 4 3 2 1

PART
ONE

1.

Gretchen Page stroked a brush through her straight blonde hair as she pressed the phone to her ear with her free hand. She tried parting her hair in the middle and letting the sides fall to her shoulders. Then she brushed some forward to see what a row of bangs might look like.

Gretchen couldn't look into a mirror without knowing her hair was her best feature. If only her olive-colored eyes were spaced a little farther apart, not so close to her nose, which she considered short and too cute and not at all elegant. And then there was that tragic tiny cleft in her chin.

She ranked herself a seven, which was good enough to be the prettiest cheerleader at Savanna Mills High. But now she was starting at Shadyside High, ten times the size of her old school, and how could she compete? There wasn't even a Sephora in Savanna Mills!

"I miss you, too, Polly," she said, fumbling the phone against her ear. She set down the hairbrush, turned away from the mirror with a sigh, crossed the bedroom, and perched on the edge of her bed. "Starting a new school junior year is the pits."

Gretchen leaned back against the big, plush Hello Kitty pillow her Grandma Hannah had given her when she was eight. A lot of the stuffing had oozed out, but she couldn't bear to part with it. Grandma Hannah was the only relative she liked.

"I always call you when the nightmares start," she told Polly. "Talking to you always makes me feel better. Yes, I had one last night. It's so sad. It was so real, so totally vivid . . . I couldn't tell if I was dreaming or not."

Gretchen sighed. "I woke up drenched in sweat. And my jaw hurt from gritting my teeth. Thank goodness I can always call you."

She shifted the phone to her other ear. "No, I haven't made any friends here," she said.

Gretchen and Polly Brown had been inseparable—like sisters—back in Savanna Mills. Their friendship went well beyond being cocaptains of the Hawks cheerleading squad.

"How could I make friends in only two weeks? The kids here aren't unfriendly. But they've all known each other for *ages*. I'm the only outsider."

She tugged at a string on the bedspread, listening to Polly's purr of a voice. She pictured Polly—round-faced with freckles and curly copper-colored hair. Polly looked about twelve—but she had a deep, sexy voice that seemed to come from deep in her throat.

"So your new school is really big?" Polly asked.

"The first few days, I couldn't even find my homeroom," Gretchen told her friend. "That's how big the school is. I mean, it's on three floors and it stretches on forever. It's like as big as the mall back home. Some kids drive from class to class!"

She listened to Polly's low chuckle. Gretchen wasn't known for her sense of humor. In fact, she was earnest and serious most of the time. But she always knew how to make Polly laugh.

"I guess it's nice to have a fresh start," Gretchen said, shifting the phone to her other ear. "And I understand why Mom had to move. I mean, after Dad left, she had to do *something*."

"True," Polly murmured. Polly never liked talking about serious, real-world troubles. She really *was* like a twelve-year-old in more than just looks.

"She got a really good deal on this house," Gretchen continued. "The real estate woman said because it's on Fear Street. I don't really get it. It's a perfectly nice street, with awesome old houses and lots of trees and big front yards."

She shifted the phone again. She realized she was squeezing it so hard, her hand ached. "My room is huge," Gretchen continued. "I even have my own bathroom, believe that? No more sharing. But I guess Fear Street is a big deal here in Shadyside. I haven't had a chance to Google it."

A cool breeze fluttered the curtains at the open bedroom window. The air chilled Gretchen's skin, an early sign of fall. Clouds covered the sun, and a gray shadow swept across the bedroom floor.

"Of course, I'm dying to make the cheerleading squad," Gretchen told Polly. "But I'm totally tense about it. Everything is so big and serious here. The high school has a real stadium behind the parking lot. Not what we had—bleachers set up on the grass."

Gretchen snickered. "No, everyone isn't rich here. It's a normal place. But they take their football seriously. The Shadyside Tigers were All-State last season. And the cheerleaders went to the state tournament and got an Honorable Mention."

"With you on the squad, they'll do better than that," Polly replied.

Gretchen sighed. "I'm not so sure about that. I've been so tense about it, I've been practicing after school all week in my backyard, believe that?"

Before Polly could answer, Gretchen's mom strode into the room, her eyes on the phone in Gretchen's hand. "Who are you talking to?"

Mrs. Page was tall and trim and athletic-looking. Back in Savanna Mills, she played tennis at her club almost every afternoon and spent at least an hour in the gym six or seven days a week.

She had short blonde hair, darker than Gretchen's, with stylish white streaks back through the sides, a broad tanned forehead, high cheekbones like a fashion model, and dark green eyes.

She was young-looking for forty-three, but Gretchen saw that the divorce and all the trouble back home had aged her. She had dark circles under her eyes, a tiny network of wrinkles on both cheeks, and even her eyes had lost some of their sparkle.

Mrs. Page made up for the change with too much makeup and too much bright orange lipstick. At least, that was Gretchen's harsh opinion.

Her mother strode quickly up to Gretchen. She wore a turquoise crewneck T-shirt over white tennis shorts that showed off her thin legs. "Gretchen, who are you talking to?" she repeated.

"None of your business," Gretchen snapped. The words came out louder than Gretchen had intended. She ended the call.

Mrs. Page let out a short gasp. "Oops. Sorry."

"Go away," Gretchen said, making a shooing motion with her free hand.

"I was just asking a simple question, Gretchen."

"Mom, what don't you understand about the words *go away*? Stop hovering over me like a drone!"

"Gretchen, think you might be overreacting a bit?"

"You can't treat me like an infant, Mom. I'm a person. I'm entitled to a little privacy. You can't barge into my room and—"

"I just want you to get off to a good start here," Mrs. Page said, suddenly breathless. She tugged the turquoise T-shirt down over her shorts. Then she ran both hands back through her short hair. "I don't think asking who you are talking to on the phone is a very big invasion of your privacy. Seriously."

Gretchen softened her glare. She nodded. "Okay. Maybe I overreacted a little." She shrugged. "Whatever."

She and her mother had always had what her mother called a *difficult* relationship. The simple fact was they hadn't gotten along since Gretchen was two and learned the word *no*.

Mrs. Page tried to show how much she cared about her daughter by involving herself in everything Gretchen did. Gretchen felt constantly smothered. The more she tried to push her away, the more Mrs. Page clung to her.

At least, that was Gretchen's side of the story.

And now that her dad had flown the coop, it was much worse.

Mrs. Page softened her expression, too. "Would you like to talk about why you overreacted?"

"Would you like to get out of my way?" Gretchen snapped. She pushed past her mother and crossed the room to her closet. She pulled out a silky maroon hoodie and swung it over her shoulder.

"Where are you going?" Mrs. Page asked.

"To school," Gretchen said, checking herself one more time in the dresser mirror.

Her mother followed her to the bedroom door. "But it's Saturday, dear."

Gretchen sighed. "I know, Mom. I have an appointment. With the cheerleading coach."

"Gretchen, just wait a minute," her mother insisted. "Just give me a minute, okay?"

Gretchen spun around in the hall. "Mom—I'll be late."

"Are you sure you want to be a cheerleader right away?"

"Excuse me? You know how important this is to me, right?"

"I'm just saying . . ." Mrs. Page hesitated. "Don't you think you should settle in first?"

"*Settle in?*" Gretchen's words burst out high and shrill. "You're joking, right? You can't be serious, Mom. Settle in? That had to be a joke."

Mrs. Page took a few steps back, as if retreating. "I'm only thinking of what's best for you, dear." She shook her head. "That's all I ever do. I just want things to go right for you. I'm not your enemy. We have to be friends. With your father gone, we have to try harder, don't you agree?"

Gretchen sighed again. "You're right, Mom. Bye."

She pounded down the stairs, taking them two at a time, and out the front door.

As she climbed behind the wheel of her mother's blue Camry, the nightmare lingered in her mind. The knife . . . the blood . . . the screams . . .

She clenched her jaw tightly. Pounded the wheel with both fists.

"Got to get past this," she said out loud. "Got to put it all behind me. Time for my fresh start.

2.

Gretchen drove to the high school. It wasn't a long drive, but she was still unfamiliar with the streets. There were probably shortcuts, but she stayed on Park Drive, which she knew cut straight through the middle of town and led to the high school at the corner of Division Street.

She could feel her heart start to beat faster as she pulled the car into the student parking lot behind the school. She didn't have a parking permit yet. But it was Saturday, so she figured no one would be checking.

As she climbed out of the car, she could hear the shouts and cries of the football team, having their afternoon practice in the stadium. She was tempted to go watch them, but she was already five minutes late for her appointment.

She trotted to the back doors of the school. It still looked immense to her. With its brick walls, faded from the sun, ivy climbing up one side, rows of tall windows, and sloping red tile roof, it looked unreal to her. Like a movie high school. Somehow high schools always looked too perfect in movies, and this one did, too.

She stepped into the back hallway. The lights had been dimmed. Silence. A ringing silence that made her stop and squint down the long, empty hallway. Gray metal lockers down both sides. Perfect. Too perfect.

Her footsteps thudded noisily as she hurried toward the front. She turned a corner and could hear the Shadyside cheerleaders practicing in the gym all the way down the hall.

She stepped under a hand-painted maroon-and-white banner that had been hung from the ceiling: TIGERS ROAR. It reminded her that the first football game was only a week away. That thought made her heartbeats race even faster.

The chanting voices from the gym grew louder as she approached. Gretchen was only a few doors away from the gym when a tall boy in faded jeans and a denim jacket burst into the hall in front of her.

She let out a startled gasp. Nearly walked right into him. "What are you doing here?" she blurted out.

"Shhhh." He raised a finger to his lips. "I'm stealing some laptops. Want to help?

3

Gretchen stared at the laptop tucked under his arm. She raised her gaze to his dark eyes. Serious eyes that crinkled up as he started to laugh. "I'm messing with you," he said. "Did you believe me?"

"I-I don't know," Gretchen stammered. She quickly got herself together. "You *do* look a lot like a thief," she joked.

He had a great smile, very warm. She liked the way his eyes crinkled up. He had short brown hair, buzzed close at the sides. The only thing that kept him from being totally awesome-looking were his ears, which stuck out like small cabbages.

"Sid Viviano," he said, introducing himself. He actually shook hands with her, and as he did his dark eyes seemed to study her face. "I'm the equipment manager for the cheerleaders."

She blinked. "Equipment manager?" They didn't have an equipment manager back in Savanna Mills.

He grinned. "I just like hanging out with a bunch of hot girls in short skirts."

"Well, at least you're honest," Gretchen said, grinning back at him.

He's very cute, and he seems to know it.

Sid raised the laptop. "I took this from the AV room. We need it for music for the practice."

"I'm late," Gretchen said, glancing at the time on her phone. "Can you tell me where Coach Walker's office is?"

"It's in the gym," he said. "This way." He motioned for her to follow him. "You're new, right? I think I saw you in Sawyer's Government class. What's your name?" He put a hand on her shoulder. "No. Wait. Let me guess. I'm good at guessing names."

He studied her for a long moment, his hand resting on her shoulder. He brought his face so close to hers, Gretchen thought he might kiss her.

Would she like that? Well . . . it was a little soon.

"I've got it. Heather," he said. "Your name is Heather, right?"

"Right," Gretchen said. "Wow. How did you do that?"

He laughed. "I just read your mind."

"Actually, my name is Gretchen. Gretchen Page."

He shook his head. "No way. *No way* do you look like a Gretchen."

"What does a Gretchen look like?"

He grinned but didn't answer.

"I'm really late," Gretchen said.

He brought his face close to hers again. His dark eyes burned into hers. "Would you like to hang out sometime?" he asked, just above a whisper.

Gretchen was about to answer when she saw the cheerleader at the gym doors. She was short and blonde and very pretty, and even from this distance, Gretchen could see that she was glaring at them angrily.

"Oh." The word slipped from Gretchen's mouth.

The girl strode up behind Sid, her face set in a scowl. She wore a maroon-and-white cheerleader uniform, a short skirt over maroon tights and a long-sleeved top with a large tiger head across the front.

Sid didn't see her until she was next to him. He was still grinning at Gretchen. His eyes widened in surprise as the girl wrapped herself around him. She draped one arm around his shoulders and pressed her face against his cheek.

As if she owns him, Gretchen thought.

"Are you Gretchen Page?" she asked, eyeing Gretchen up and down.

Gretchen nodded. "Yes. Sorry I'm late. I—"

"I'm Stacy Grande. I'm the cheerleading captain." She laughed. Her blue eyes flashed. "Did you think you could get a spot on the squad by flirting with my boyfriend?"

Gretchen could feel her face grow hot and knew she was blushing. She was one of those people who blushed easily, blushed all the time, often for no big reason at all, and she hated that about herself. It embarrassed her so that she blushed even darker.

"I-I wasn't flirting," she stammered. "I'm . . . late." She brushed past Sid and Stacy and vanished into the gym.

"Well . . . *that* went well," she muttered.

Not a good start. But she had no way of knowing her troubles had just begun.

4.

Coach Walker's office stood at the far end of a row of small glass-windowed offices along one side of the gym. The cheerleaders, Gretchen saw, had taken a break from their practice. They were perched in the bleachers, water bottles in one hand, phones in the other.

Through the glass window, Gretchen could see that two girls were already in Walker's office, seated in front of the cluttered desk, both talking animatedly. Gretchen hesitated outside the door, unsure whether to go in or wait.

Coach Walker was a tall, lean black woman. She was dressed in purple sweats and had a blue-and-white Yankees cap over her short hair. She saw Gretchen through the glass, stood up, and opened the office door. "Are you Gretchen? I'm Coach Walker."

Gretchen nodded. "Sorry I'm late."

"No worries. I'll be right back." Walker was at least a foot taller than Gretchen. She turned and jogged to the gym doors.

The two girls in the office both stared intently at Gretchen. She swept her hair back with both hands and entered the office to introduce herself.

"I'm Devra Dalby," said one of the girls. She had beautiful, wavy red hair and creamy white skin, unreal skin, Gretchen noticed immediately. Her blue eyes were large and round and icy cold. And she had an amused little grin on her face even though Gretchen didn't see anything to be amused about. "And this is my friend Courtney Shaw."

Courtney was in a cheerleader uniform. She had very short black hair, shaved close on one side. She had a slender face, gray eyes surrounded by a lot of dark eye makeup, a short turned-up nose, a silver ring in one nostril.

Courtney had the same amused look on her face as Devra. As if the two of them shared a joke.

Am I the joke? Gretchen wondered.

"I like your outfit," Devra said. "Nice hoodie."

The girls exchanged glances. Gretchen caught their vibe. They were laughing at her for some reason.

"Coach Walker said you were from Savanna Mills," Devra said. "Is that really a place? It sounds made up."

She and Courtney laughed, as if that was a great joke.

"It's a real place," Gretchen said. "But if you blink, you miss it."

"Small towns are the best," Courtney said to Devra, her eyes flashing.

"If you're a small town person. . . ." Devra added. She

changed to a funny voice and did a short dialogue. " 'Want to hang out at the 7-Eleven tonight?' 'Huh? The 7-Eleven? That's too exciting. How about the DQ?' "

Gretchen watched them laugh. *How do I win them over? They're both so snotty.*

Devra's smile faded. Her blue eyes turned icy. She had a red-and-yellow bandanna tied tightly over her fore-head. She untied it, then tied it again. "Listen, Gretch," she said, peering out to see if Coach Walker was returning. "If you've come for the cheerleader position, it's already taken—by *me*."

The two girls didn't wait for Gretchen to reply. They both jumped up and hurried out of the office. Gretchen could feel that her face was still hot. Without realizing it, she had balled her hands into fists. She watched the two girls as they crossed the gym to the bleachers.

But her eyes wandered to the wall at the side of the bleachers. She saw Sid and Stacy. Sid had his arms around Stacy's waist, and they were locked in a long kiss.

To Gretchen's surprise, Devra stopped halfway across the gym floor. Her mouth dropped open as she watched Sid and Stacy against the wall.

Why does Devra suddenly look so angry? Gretchen won-dered. *She looks as if she wants to kill them both.*

5.

A few minutes later, Coach Walker returned to her office. She dropped behind her desk and slid her phone onto the desktop. She adjusted the Yankees cap over her hair. Gretchen saw that she had tiny diamond studs on both sides of her nose.

"Sorry to keep you waiting. Did you meet Devra and Courtney?"

Gretchen nodded. "Yes. We . . . uh . . . talked for a bit." She clasped her hands tightly in her lap, surprised to find them damp and ice cold.

"Your family just moved to Shadyside?"

Gretchen nodded again. "My mom and me. A few weeks ago."

Coach Walker toyed with the silver whistle that dangled from her neck. "How are you finding it?"

"Big," Gretchen said.

That made the coach smile for the first time. But the

smile faded quickly. "I'm afraid your timing is bad. We had only one position to fill, and I just gave it to Devra."

Gretchen couldn't hide her disappointment. She let out a long sigh.

"Devra was the alternate last year," Coach Walker said. "So I thought she should move onto the squad for this year."

"But . . ." Gretchen fumbled in her bag and pulled out the disc she had brought. "I have a highlight reel," she said, raising it to the coach. "Maybe if you have time, you can watch. . . ."

Coach Walker took the disk from her. "Is this video from your old school?"

"Yes. I was cocaptain. The school was smaller, but we had six girls on the squad, just like here."

Coach Walker studied the disc for a moment. She smiled again. "Why don't we watch it now?"

She pulled a disc drive from a bottom desk drawer and plugged it into her laptop. Then she motioned for Gretchen to slide her chair around to her side of the desk so they could watch it together.

As the video started and Gretchen watched the Savanna Mills cheerleaders run onto the floor to start their routines, she felt a pang of sadness. She watched Polly do a series of cartwheels across the floor. She liked all these girls. They had so much fun together. They were a real *team.*

The girls suddenly looked so young to Gretchen. She

had the weird feeling she was watching an old movie. Something that happened far away in a different time.

Can't let the sadness take over. . . .

She raised her gaze to Coach Walker, who was watching the routines intently. "Good. Very good," she murmured. She turned to Gretchen. "Very good L Stand to a Shoulder Sit. That's so basic, but you made it look fresh."

"Thanks," Gretchen said. "I think the Thigh Stand is next."

Coach Walker turned her attention back to the laptop screen. "Yes. That's impressive," she said, nodding her head. "Both Thigh Stands are perfect. And I like your smile, Gretchen. I like the way you make it look as if you are enjoying yourself."

"Well . . . actually, I *was*," Gretchen said.

Coach Walker stopped the video. "I'm impressed."

Gretchen felt her heartbeat start to race again. "Thank you. I do a Flying Somersault at the end. It's kind of my specialty."

"I'm going to watch the whole thing later," the coach said. "Have you met Stacy? She's our captain. I want her to watch it, too."

"I met her. Out in the hall," Gretchen said. Then she thought: *And Stacy thought I was flirting with her boyfriend.*

"Tell you what, Gretchen," Coach Walker said, twirling the silver whistle. "Devra isn't going to like this, but I'm going to let you try out. I think this team has a chance of going to the state tournament. And I want it to have only the best cheerleaders we have in school. I think you're really good, and it's only fair to give you a chance to make the squad."

Gretchen's heart skipped a beat. She wanted to jump up and hug Coach Walker. "Oh . . . thank you," she managed to say.

Walker jumped to her feet. "I have to tell Devra right away." She saw Devra sitting beside Courtney at the far end of the bleachers. She cupped her hands around her mouth and shouted for Devra to come to the office.

Devra entered the office with her arms crossed in front of her, a suspicious look on her face. Coach Walker motioned for her to take the chair next to Gretchen. "Change of plans," the coach said.

Devra's blue eyes grew wider. She adjusted her red-and-yellow bandanna and flipped back her wavy, red hair with a toss of her head.

Coach Walker hesitated. She took a breath. "I've decided to give Gretchen a chance to try out for the position on the squad," she said. Both of her hands gripped the edge of her desktop, as if she expected a torrent of protest.

Devra yawned.

She squinted at Coach Walker. "What did you just say?"

"I said we want the best talent we can get on the squad," the coach replied. "So I've given Gretchen a chance to try out."

Devra's eyes flashed. She glared at Gretchen, a hard, angry stare.

But then she said in a voice just above a whisper, "No worries. No worries at all."

A few minutes later, Gretchen was driving home, singing along to the radio, the music cranked way up. She roared up Park Drive, made a squealing turn into a street she didn't know, singing and laughing, and feeling the joy of being a winner.

She sailed through several blocks, the houses and cars a colorful blur sweeping past the windshield. Stopping for a light, she cut off the music and pulled out her phone. She pushed Polly's number to tell her the good news.

"I know I can beat Devra Dalby," she told her old friend. "I know I can make this squad. You should have seen the coach's face. She was definitely impressed. And I'm impressed with her. I think it took courage to give this girl Devra the news. Devra seems to be some kind of tiger."

Gretchen turned back onto Park Drive. "Hard to believe, Polly, but I made *two* enemies in one day. Stacy and Devra. But they'll get over it. I'm sure they will."

Gretchen let out a shocked scream as a gunshot—a deafening *crack* of sound—rang out right behind her. Her hands flew up, the phone fell to the floor, and the car squealed out of control.

6.

Gretchen's foot slammed the brake. She grabbed the wheel and twisted it as the car slid toward a light pole at the curb. A low moan escaped her throat as the car bumped onto the curb, jolting her whole body, and came to a stop an inch from the pole.

A shrill wail rose up around her. It took her a few seconds to realize she was leaning on the horn. Struggling to catch her breath, Gretchen gripped the wheel again and pressed her back against the car seat.

A close one.

Her hand trembled as she pushed open the door. She leaned over and saw the flat tire even before she climbed out. The front tire on the driver's side. It spread flat on the pavement.

A blowout. Not a gunshot. A tire blowout.

She stared at it until it blurred in front of her eyes.

You're just tense because the nightmares have returned, she told herself. *You have got to get your imagination under control.*

A few miles away in North Hills, the expensive neighborhood of Shadyside, Devra Dalby leaned forward on the leather desk chair in her bedroom and gazed at her father on her laptop screen. "Dad, the only way I see you these days is on FaceTime," she said.

He frowned. "I know. Inventory time is always crazy. And we've had board meetings all week to make matters worse." He rubbed his eyes wearily.

He's looking older, Devra realized. Why hadn't she noticed the gray that had crept into the sides of his hair and the dark lines under his eyes? Was it because he was never home?

Her dad had always prided himself on being the energetic, dynamic, handsome Dalby. His two brothers were no match for him. They helped him run the department store chain, but they were just helpers, and everyone knew it.

As CEO of the Dalby stores, he wore $2,000 suits and wore them well. He had a collection of Rolex watches and a hundred Ferragamo neckties. Everything he wore had to be the best. He said it was important since he represented the image of the stores.

He kept himself in excellent shape. He had two personal trainers who came to the house. The gym in the basement was state-of-the-art.

But here he was looking tired, and it wasn't just the bad lighting on the laptop screen. Devra had always thought of him as a young George Clooney. The resemblance was definitely there. But leaning forward with her elbows on her desk, studying him now as he sat behind the wide glass desk in his office, his cheeks were puffy and his eyes were bloodshot.

"Gretchen, what's up?" he said, unable to hide his impatience. He never liked a conversation to last more than five minutes.

"A little problem at school," Devra told him. She pushed back her hair with both hands. "I told you how I was being promoted to cheerleader, remember? Coach Walker said I could have the position? Well . . . this new girl marched in and is messing everything up."

Mr. Dalby turned away from the screen for a moment and called something to someone who had entered his office. Then he turned back to the camera. "Messed everything up?"

Devra nodded. "Yeah. Now Walker changed her mind and is letting this new girl try out."

Mr. Dalby rubbed his chin. "That doesn't seem right."

"Of *course* it isn't right," Devra snapped. "She promised me the position on the squad. I was an alternate all last year, right? I earned it, Dad."

"Okay, okay. Don't shout, Devra."

"Sorry. But I'm so steamed. This new girl . . . Gretchen Something-Or-Other . . . with her blonde hair

29

and big olive eyes . . . AAARRRGH. You know I need this, Dad. I need the extra-curricular points to get into Princeton."

"I know, I know," Mr. Dalby said softly. He let out a long whoosh of air. "Try to calm down. . . ."

"Calm down?" Devra cried. "What if she's really good? What if she's better than me? Does that mean I spend another year as an alternate? That's unacceptable. Seriously. That's unacceptable, Dad."

"Devra, you're shouting," Mr. Dalby said. He drummed his fingers on the glass desktop. "Listen. Maybe I can make a call to the principal. Mr. Hernandez. You know I donate a lot of money to the school development fund every year. That has to count for something, don't you think?"

"It better," Devra muttered.

"Well . . . I can't promise anything. But—"

"Call him, Dad. We can't let this new girl do this to me. It just isn't fair."

"Okay. I'll see what I can do."

"I really miss you. When are you coming home?"

Mr. Dalby shrugged. "I'm in Chicago tomorrow. Then Toronto. Then there's a meeting of all the buyers." He adjusted his tie with both hands. "Did Courtney move in with you? To keep you company?"

Devra nodded. "Yes. She's here. I put her in the blue guestroom across from my room."

"Good. That's good. What are you two up to?"

30

Devra leaned toward the camera on top of the lap-top. "We're already plotting ways to kill this new girl. Gretchen."

Mr. Dalby laughed. "Well, don't kill her yet. Let me make a friendly call to Mr. Hernandez first."

7.

Gretchen groaned as she started her stretching exercises in the backyard. She thought she might do some jogging around the neighborhood. She had never been a runner, but she really needed to work off some nervous energy.

Her leg muscles felt tight. She knew that thinking about the cheerleader tryout was making her tense. She had a stupid fight with her mother that morning. She couldn't even remember what it was about. Something about too much milk making her breakfast cereal soggy?

It was warm, the sun high in the afternoon sky, a summer day lingering into September. She exercised on the small square patio outside the kitchen door. Weeds poked up through the cracks, and many of the flagstones were cracked and broken.

Gretchen's new backyard was wide but not very deep. At the side of the two-car garage, a long, bare dirt patch stretched where there obviously had been a flower garden.

The back of the yard was marked by a low wooden fence with several missing slats and badly in need of a paint job.

Mrs. Page said she didn't want to deal with the yard at all, not until spring, not until they'd made the house livable. Gretchen didn't really care. But her yard sure looked shabby next to the neighbor's yard, which was mowed smooth and low without a single protruding weed, and had a long row of late-blooming red pansies running the length of an evergreen hedge at the far side of the property.

Gazing at the neighbor's yard, Gretchen suddenly heard violin music. Running scales followed by a short melody. It wasn't the first time she had heard it. She turned to the house next door and, squinting against the sunlight off a side window, saw a girl in the house, a violin on her shoulder.

The girl swung her head and shoulders as she played. She appeared to be staring out at Gretchen. When she flashed a smile, Gretchen stood up, pulled down her sweatshirt, and trotted toward the girl's kitchen door.

The girl met Gretchen at the door. She smiled, holding the violin and bow at her side. "Hey, you're the new neighbor," she said. "I've seen you in school."

Gretchen introduced herself. "I've heard you playing before."

"Hope it isn't too loud. I usually keep the window closed. But it's such a beautiful warm day. . . . I'm

Madison, by the way. Madison Grossman. I'm in another eleventh-grade homeroom. Mr. Bartleby. I saw that
you're across the hall. Do you drive? We could drive to
school together."

"I drive sometimes. My mom usually needs the car,"
Gretchen said.

Madison spoke rapidly, very precisely, without seeming
to take a breath. She was very thin, birdlike, with very
curly black hair down to her shoulders, dark, close-
together eyes over a sharp, almost pointed nose. Her skin
was pale, almost colorless, as if she never went outside.

She wore an orange crewneck T-shirt over a short
black skirt over black tights.

She stepped aside and motioned with the violin bow
for Gretchen to come inside. "I'm in the school orchestra. Did you know Shadyside High had a symphony orchestra? We're pretty good, actually. Mr. Colon—he's the
advisor—used to be with the Detroit Symphony. We give
two full concerts a year. Last year we did a concert at
the Vets Memorial Theater in Martinsville, and we sold
the place out."

"That's awesome," Gretchen said. She followed Madison into a small den of dark green walls and brown leather
armchairs and a couch.

A large oil painting stood over the green marble fireplace. It showed a nine- or ten-year-old girl with black
curly hair, holding a violin to her neck. "That's me,"
Madison said. "My mom paints a little. Well, more than

a little. She has a studio down in the basement. She's down there all the time. She isn't a name or anything yet. But she's actually sold some of her paintings."

Gretchen gazed at the painting and laughed. "You haven't changed very much."

Madison laughed, too. Pink circles formed on her pale cheeks. "Ha. I guess you're right. I have kind of a baby face."

"And you were playing violin when you were little?"

Madison nodded. "My parents started me on a Suzuki kids' violin program when I was three. I thought I'd hate it, but I was some kind of prodigy, you know. I mean, I loved it right away."

"You must practice a lot," Gretchen said, her eyes still on the girl in the painting.

"I've seen you practicing, too," Madison said. "Cheerleader stuff." She blushed again. "I wasn't spying or anything. It's just that our backyards connect and—"

"I'm trying out for the cheerleader squad," Gretchen interrupted. "Coach Walker is giving me a chance. Since I just started at school."

"You were a cheerleader before?"

Gretchen nodded. "I was cocaptain at my old school. We were really good. I'm not just bragging. We got a lot of attention. They have cheerleading scholarships at some colleges I'm interested in. It's really important for me to make the squad."

Gretchen realized she was chattering as much as Madison. But Madison seemed so easy to talk to. It didn't happen to Gretchen often, but once in a while, she found someone she clicked with, someone like Polly, on her wavelength, someone she felt immediately comfortable with.

Madison brought some bottles of iced tea from the kitchen, and they sat across from each other in the den, talking and getting to know one another. After about half an hour, Madison glanced at the old-fashioned-looking wooden clock on the corner of the mantel.

She jumped to her feet. "Wow. I almost forgot. I have to go try on a dress I bought. It's for my cousin's bar mitzvah, and I promised my Mom I'd go try it on today."

Gretchen followed her toward the front door. "Well . . . nice to meet you. I'll see you in school and—"

"Hey, want to come along?" Madison asked.

Gretchen stopped walking. "Where are you going?"

"To the department store. It will only take ten minutes."

"Well, actually, I need to buy some things," Gretchen said. "I need tights. And some new workout clothes." She tugged at the top of her shorts. "Look at this. The elastic is all stretched."

Madison picked up a set of car keys from the table in the front entryway. "So you're coming?"

"Let me get changed into some jeans, and I'll be right back."

Gretchen ran full speed back to her house. *Madison is really nice,* she thought. *Maybe I've made a new friend.*

She felt happy for the first time since arriving in Shadyside. She had no idea how much trouble a visit to a department store could cause.

8.

Madison played a classical music Pandora station as they drove to the Division Street Mall. "I like new music, too," she said. "But this perfect for driving. It's so quiet and calm."

Gretchen nodded. Her family didn't listen to classical music. Gretchen seldom ventured from the top hits stations.

At the far end of the mall, the department store loomed high over the other buildings. Madison parked and they entered from a side entrance, into the bargain basement department.

Gretchen followed Madison onto an Up escalator, and they traveled to the first floor. Gretchen took a deep breath. The heavy perfumed air washed over her. The cosmetics department stretched as far as she could see, the floor brighter than daylight. Glass counters reflected the light. Videos played on big flatscreens. Women leaned on the counters or arranged the products, or chatted among each other, or sprayed passersby with perfumes and cologne scents.

"We had a Sears and a Kmart," Gretchen told Madison. "But nothing as big as this. Or as modern. Or as crowded."

Then she stopped and grabbed Madison's arm when she recognized a girl behind a makeup counter. "Hey—!" A cry escaped her throat. She stared at Devra Dalby.

"Madison, what's *she* doing here?" Gretchen asked.

Madison followed her gaze. "You mean Devra? What's she doing here? You're joking, right? This is *her* store. Her family owns all the Dalby stores."

Gretchen's head was suddenly spinning. "I-I didn't see the name when we came in," she stammered.

"Devra's grandfather opened this store," Madison continued. "Now there are like dozens of them all over. Devra is richer than anyone in Shadyside—and she acts it!"

Devra didn't see them. They both watched her disappear around the back of the counter. Gretchen breathed a long sigh. She knew Devra hated her, or at least, resented her. She didn't want to have an encounter with her here in front of Madison.

"I took her spot on the squad away," Gretchen tried to explain to Madison. "I mean, Coach Walker gave it to her, then changed her mind. She's letting us both try out, and only one of us will get the spot."

Madison did an exaggerated shudder. "Trouble," she murmured. "I wouldn't mess with Devra."

"You mean—"

"I got into a fight with her on the playground in second grade," Madison said. "She was a beast. She grabbed my hair and wouldn't let go. The teacher couldn't even pry her hands off me. She's relentless. I mean, she's psycho. And you know what? She hasn't spoken to me since. Do you believe that? The fight was in second grade, and she still holds a grudge."

"Wow." Gretchen shook her head. "Wow." A thousand frightening thoughts flashed through her mind. "Madison, you don't really think she's *dangerous,* do you?"

Madison shrugged. Gretchen couldn't read her expression. Madison suddenly seemed to be far away. "I'll meet you downstairs where we came in," she said, starting down the aisle. "Half an hour?"

Gretchen nodded. She watched her new friend walk past the cosmetics counters toward the back of the store. Then she gazed around quickly, looking for Devra, glad she wasn't there.

A few minutes later, she was checking out workout tights in a large athletic-wear department on the second floor. The shelves of running shoes and sneakers covered one wall from floor to ceiling. An old Rolling Stones song blared from hidden ceiling speakers. People in the crowded aisle seemed to move in rhythm with the music.

Beat. Beat. Beat.

Gretchen spotted another display of tights near the far wall. She squeezed past a young couple with a baby stroller, turned toward the display—and bumped hard into a boy.

They both stumbled, off-balance. He grabbed her by the arms and steadied her. And she recognized Sid Viviano. Stacy's boyfriend. Sid from school. Sid the cheerleader equipment manager. Holding her by the arms, a broad smile on his handsome face.

Did he bump into me deliberately?

"Hey," he said. "That was like a head-on collision. Are you okay?"

Gretchen felt her face growing hot. She eased her arms free of his grip. "Yeah. Fine. Hi. How's it going?"

"Not bad." His grin didn't fade. His eyes locked on hers. He appeared to be studying her intently, like trying to dig into her brain.

"What are you doing here?" Gretchen blurted out.

"Ha. Stalking you."

"No. Really."

He pointed. "There were these awesome new Air Jordans. I thought I'd check them out. But . . . you have to be a millionaire. No way I could afford them."

"I . . . I'm just getting some workout stuff," Gretchen said. "This store is so big. Back home, we—" She stopped. His stare was starting to make her feel uncomfortable. "Sid, why are you staring at me like that?"

His smile finally faded. His eyes flashed. "That day I met you . . ." he started. "In the hall outside the gym, remember? I . . . I kind of felt there was something between us." He grabbed her arms again. "Did you feel it, too?"

Gretchen tried to back away. *This is too intense.* But there was something so attractive about him. A kind of power. An aura that drew her to him like an invisible magnet.

And now he was pushing her against the display table, tightening his arms around her.

"Sid—no. I don't think—"

She started to protest. But now she was kissing him back. He was holding her, pressing her against the table . . . kissing her, his lips hard against hers.

And as they kissed, her eyes traveled to the mirror on the floor. She gazed into the reflection—and saw Devra Dalby watching . . . watching them . . . her features twisted in an ugly scowl.

9.

efty's, the Home of the Two-Dollar Double Cheeseburger, was conveniently located across from Shadyside High and instantly became a popular hangout. Madison had a seven o'clock violin lesson on Tuesday nights, so Gretchen met her there a little before six for an early dinner.

Madison slid into the red vinyl booth at the back wall of the restaurant and carefully tucked her violin case beside her. She gave her head a hard shake, sending her curly hair into place around her head.

Gretchen shivered and tugged down the sleeves of her sweater. The weather had turned cool but, for some reason, Lefty's still had its air conditioner going.

The waitress said hello and set down the yellow-and-red menus. The menus were short. There were few choices other than cheeseburgers.

"How's it going, Rachel?" Madison asked the waitress. "Gretchen, do you know Rachel Martin? She's a senior."

Gretchen and Rachel exchanged hellos.

"Tuesdays are quiet," Rachel told Madison, motioning around the restaurant. "That's good and bad. I don't have to work so hard, but the tips are really lame."

Madison tsk-tsked. "What's the special tonight?"

"Cheeseburgers."

All three of the girls laughed. *Rachel seems nice,* Gretchen thought, turning back to Madison. She had a question she was eager to ask her.

But Madison started talking first, chattering on in her rapid-fire way. "I'm totally tense. I didn't sleep last night."

"What's wrong?"

"I don't think I mentioned it, but my mom is on the school board. She arranged for a very famous string quartet to come play for an assembly at school."

"Nice," Gretchen said.

Madison frowned. "Let me finish. Mom also arranged for them to let *me* sit in with them onstage for one of the pieces. That would make me nervous enough. But it's a Bach piece I just started to learn." Madison shook her shoulders. "I'm shaking just talking about it now. Seriously."

Gretchen patted Madison's hand. "No worries. You'll be great."

"How do you know that?" Madison snapped.

"I don't," Gretchen replied. "I didn't know what else to say. I was trying to be nice. Maybe you'll suck in front of the whole school."

That made Madison laugh. "You're funny." She shifted the violin case beside her. "My violin teacher is going to give me some hints on how to learn the piece. But I need more than hints. I need faster fingers and a faster brain."

"I was at my cousin Marty's house a few years ago," Gretchen said, "and he made me watch this horror movie about a violin player. The musician had his hand chopped off, and the hand continued to play the violin on its own."

Madison narrowed her eyes at Gretchen. "And you're suggesting . . . ?"

They both laughed.

Rachel Martin returned and set down the cheeseburgers and fries they had ordered. "Do you need mustard or mayo or anything?"

Both girls said no.

Rachel lingered, her eyes on Gretchen. "I hear you made a new friend your first week in school."

Gretchen squinted at her. "Excuse me?"

A thin smile crossed Rachel's face. "Devra Dalby?"

"You're being sarcastic?" Gretchen said.

Rachel nodded. "Yes. I'm being sarcastic. Devra was talking about you at lunch yesterday. I don't think she's a fan." She leaned toward Gretchen. "What did you do to tick her off?"

"Showed up," Gretchen said.

Lefty rang the bell at the kitchen window. Rachel hurried away. She had more cheeseburgers to deliver.

Gretchen lifted the top half of the bun and dabbed some ketchup on her cheeseburger. "I want to ask you something about Devra," she told Madison.

Madison snickered. "I'm not exactly a Devra expert, you know. I told you, we don't speak to one another." She cut her cheeseburger in half and lifted one of the halves in both hands.

"Did Devra ever go out with Sid?" Gretchen asked.

Madison lowered the cheeseburger to the plate. "Huh?"

"Did she ever have a thing about Sid? Do you know if they ever went out together?"

"It's possible." Madison took a bite of the cheeseburger and chewed for a while, looking thoughtful. "Sid has had a lot of girlfriends. He's a definite chick magnet." She giggled. "I read that phrase in a really bad romance novel."

"But before Stacy—?" Gretchen started.

"I don't think he and Devra were ever a thing. And now he and Stacy are like the perfect couple. At least, *they* seem to think so."

Both girls concentrated on their food for a while. Then Madison asked, "Why did you ask me about Devra and Sid?"

Gretchen wiped grease off her chin with a napkin. "I saw her a couple of times, and when Sid was around, she got this unhappy look on her face. I mean, he was kissing Stacy in the gym, and Devra just stopped and scowled at them."

"Weird," Madison murmured. She glanced at her phone. "Oh, wow. I'm going to be late." She grabbed the violin case and started to slide out of the booth. "Can you get this?"

"Sure, I'll pay," Gretchen said.

"My treat next time."

"Talk to you later?"

"If I survive Bach!" Madison called. Then she was out the door.

Gretchen gazed after her. The restaurant became a bright blur. Loud voices and clinking plates and shouts from the kitchen and the slam of the door. She couldn't get Devra out of her mind. She kept seeing all these vague images of Devra's cold, unhappy face. Like a swirling nightmare, only Gretchen was awake.

And when Devra actually slid into the booth across from her, Gretchen nearly screamed.

10.

O h. Sorry," Devra said. "Did I scare you?"

"No. I . . . uh . . . was daydreaming," Gretchen managed to say.

Gretchen stared at the necklace that swung down from Devra's throat, large jewel-like blue beads, a little darker than the blue designer top she wore. Her red hair was pulled back in a single braid. Gretchen couldn't help but notice how creamy and perfect her skin was under the harsh ceiling lights.

Devra's thin smile revealed that startling Gretchen had pleased her.

Gretchen lowered her eyes to Devra's hand. Two of her fingers were heavily wrapped in bandages. "What happened to your hand?" she asked.

Devra held it up. "Acid burns. Believe it?"

Gretchen blinked. "Excuse me? Acid? How—?"

Devra lowered the hand to her lap. She rolled her eyes. "I don't know where I get these crazy ideas. There's an antique cabinet my dad loves. It was painted badly, and the paint is cracking. I decided to refinish it for him. For his birthday. I'm going to surprise him with it."

"And the acid?" Gretchen said.

"I'm using this kind of acid to remove the old paint. They showed me how to use it at the home crafts store. But I had trouble opening the bottle and . . ." She raised the hand again. "It burned so bad. Do you believe our housekeeper had to drive me to the emergency room?"

"Whoa. That's horrible," Gretchen said.

Devra rolled her eyes again. "Dad will love the cabinet . . . . If he ever sees it. He's away a lot."

What does she want? Gretchen wondered. *She didn't sit down to discuss her cabinet. Or her father. Is she going to ask me about kissing Sid in the department store?*

"I want to talk to you," Devra said, burying the bandaged hand in her lap. "You're just a junior, right?"

Gretchen nodded. "Yeah." She gazed down at her half-uneaten cheeseburger. Her stomach was twisted in knots now. She knew she'd never finish it.

"Well, I'm a senior," Devra said. "This is my last chance, you know?"

Gretchen squinted at her. "What do you mean?"

"I mean, this is my last chance to make the cheerleading squad. Because I'll be gone next year."

Gretchen nodded. She realized she had her suddenly icy hands clasped tightly in her lap. "So?"

Devra leaned across the table. "So maybe we can

make a deal." When Gretchen didn't respond to that, Devra continued. "I don't know if you're any good or not. I guess Coach Walker thought you were good enough to compete with me. But—"

"Can I get you anything else?" Rachel Martin reappeared at the table.

"You could try not interrupting people," Devra snapped.

Rachel blushed. "Sorry. I—"

"Just the check, please," Gretchen said.

Devra waited for Rachel to leave. "All I'm saying is, let me win the tryout tomorrow. You'll be an alternate. Chances are, you'll get to fill in for somebody. You'll be with the squad the whole year. Then I'll graduate and go happily away. And it'll be all yours."

Gretchen suddenly realized that her mouth had dropped open. She was staring at Devra in disbelief. Devra's words kept repeating in Gretchen's mind. She just couldn't get her head around what Devra was asking her.

Deliberately blow the tryout?

"I . . . don't . . . think . . . so," she managed to say.

Devra let out a whoosh of air. She couldn't hide her frustration. Gretchen saw that she wasn't used to people saying no to her.

"Devra, I can't fail on purpose tomorrow," she said softly, clasping her hands together even more tightly. "Coach Walker saw my highlight reel. She saw what I can do. If I suddenly turned into a klutz . . ."

Devra's eyes flashed angrily. "What would it take to change your mind? How about a five-hundred-dollar credit at Dalby's?"

Gretchen gasped. "Are you actually bribing me?"

"Think of the outfits you could buy, Gretchen. You could upgrade your whole wardrobe. You wouldn't have to wear those Old Navy rejects."

"That's disgusting!" Gretchen cried. "Do you really think you can get anything you want by paying people? By using your family's store to—"

"How about a thousand-dollar store credit?" Devra interrupted. "Just stop and think about it."

"No way." Gretchen realized her whole body was trembling, trembling in anger. "I can't believe this is happening," she said. "I can't believe you would stoop so low. How can it be so important to you, Devra?"

"I need it for college," Devra replied through gritted teeth. Her cheeks were bright pink. Her features were tight with anger. "Listen to me—"

"No. I'm going to try my hardest at the tryout," Gretchen insisted. "And if I'm better than you—"

Devra leaned close and practically spit her next words in Gretchen's ear. "You wouldn't want Stacy to know about that little love scene you had at the store with her boyfriend—would you?"

Gretchen pulled her head back. She crossed her arms in front of her, as if shielding herself. "No way. No way.

No way. I won't do it." Her heart was pounding so hard, she felt dizzy.

Devra didn't reply. She just nodded. She slid out of the booth and glared down at Gretchen. "You'll regret this. I promise."

"Good luck at the tryout," Gretchen said.

Devra sneered at her. "Break a leg."

11.

Home alone. Gretchen slumped back on the soft leather of the living room couch and listened to the rattle of a tree branch against the front window. Her mom knew the front yard trees had to be cut back. The limbs had grown dangerously close to the house. But that problem wasn't at the top of her list.

Gretchen pressed her hands into the cushion and listened to the *tap-tap-tap*. It sounded like someone knocking on the window, trying to get in.

Don't freak yourself out, she scolded herself. She'd felt tense, totally on edge since her confrontation with Devra an hour earlier. She kept playing the conversation over again in her mind.

Each time it made her angrier—and more anxious about how desperate Devra was to win the cheerleader spot this year.

"Spoiled brat," Gretchen murmured out loud. Obviously, Devra was used to getting whatever she wanted.

Gretchen sighed. Didn't Devra realize how lucky she was? Her father owned department stores. He and Devra lived in North Hills. Madison had explained to her that was the fanciest section of Shadyside, with enormous mansions, gated to keep the rest of the world out.

Gretchen's father had moved to Milwaukee with his new girlfriend. He didn't care if he heard from Gretchen or not. He never tried to call her or even email. Not a word from him on her last birthday.

She shifted tensely on the couch, listening to the insistent *tap-tap-tap* at the window. The house was silent. So silent she heard the *click* of the fridge rumbling on in the kitchen.

With a sigh, she raised her phone. Maybe Madison was back from her violin lesson. She wanted to tell her about Devra's attempt to bribe her. She listened to the ring until Madison's voicemail came on. Then she clicked it off.

Gretchen realized her hands were shaking.

Why am I so upset?

I'm too old to be scared of being home alone.

She knew it wasn't that. She had looked forward to a new start here in Shadyside. A house on Fear Street sounded intriguing, even exciting. Why would someone give a street that name?

It wasn't being home alone in a new house on a windy night that disturbed her. It was Devra Dalby. Once again, she pictured Devra's head toss, sending her red hair back over her shoulders . . . her icy blue eyes. . . .

Devra's harsh whisper: *"How about a thousand-dollar store credit?"*

Gretchen squeezed the phone in her hand. *Maybe I'll call Polly. Talking to Polly always helps me get my head together.*

Just as Gretchen started to push Polly's number, the doorbell rang.

A loud *clang clang*.

Gretchen jumped, startled. She hadn't heard the doorbell before. No one had visited yet.

She set down the phone and earphones and strode to the front entryway. She frowned at the framed color print her mother had hung on the entry wall—six dogs wearing human clothes, sitting around a card table playing poker.

"Just a joke," Mrs. Page had explained. "Until our real art arrives from Savanna Mills."

Gretchen thought it embarrassing that her mother had even *bought* something so atrocious.

The bell clanged again. "Who is it?" Gretchen called, her throat clogged from not talking to anyone for an hour.

No answer.

"Who's there?"

Gretchen pulled the door. It stuck. The wood had swollen, making it too tight against the frame. Another fix-it project on her mother's list. She gave it a hard tug with both hands, and it swung open.

Gretchen stared into the triangle of yellow light from the porchlight.

No one there.

"Hello?" she called. "Hey—are you there?"

The wind made the trees shake. Dead leaves rained to the ground. The lawn was already covered in a blanket of fallen leaves. Gusts of wind made a whispering sound all around.

Gretchen squinted to the street. No cars. No one there. A quick glance at the front of Madison's house next-door. No one.

With a shiver, she shoved the door closed. She stood in the entryway, staring at the hideous dog print on the wall. *The wind couldn't have rung the doorbell.*

A hard tap on the front window made Gretchen spin around. It seemed louder than the gentle tapping of the tree branch.

Another hard knock. Another. Was someone pounding on the window?

Gretchen lurched back into the living room. She tripped over the edge of the carpet that hadn't been tacked down yet. Caught her balance. Eyes on the window. Only darkness beyond the pale curtain of light from the front porch.

She pushed her nose against the cold glass and peered out.

No one there.

Is this a joke? Or am I going crazy?

The hard, repeated knock on the kitchen door made her cry out. The sound rang down the back hallway. Definitely a fist pounding on the glass section of the back door.

"Who is it?" Gretchen shouted. Sudden fear tightened her throat as she ran through the hall, shoes thudding loudly on the bare floorboards. "Who's there?"

Into the kitchen. A single ceiling light on dim. Neat and clean. No one had eaten at home tonight.

A drumlike pounding on the door. Gretchen saw only darkness in the glass square that formed the top half of the door.

She grabbed the knob. Breathless. Heartbeats racing now. Grabbed the knob with both hands and yanked the door open.

A whoosh of cold air greeted her. "Who's there? Who is doing this?"

A lawn rake on its side against the back stoop. The wooden lawn chairs and table glowing dully under the light of a half-moon.

No one there. And no footsteps. No one running to the side of the house.

A ghost.

Gretchen allowed herself a stupid thought. *Yes, a ghost. That must be why they call this Fear Street.*

She still held the knob to the kitchen door in her hand when she heard the *clang* of the front doorbell.

Someone is playing a mean joke.

Someone is trying to scare me. And it's working.

She slammed the kitchen door and carefully locked it. She checked the kitchen window. Locked.

The doorbell rang again.

Gretchen stopped halfway down the back hall. *I'm not going into the living room. I'm not going to answer it.*

Her whole body shuddered. Did someone plan to break in? Or were they just trying to terrorize her? Such a mean, babyish stunt. But she had no way of knowing if it was just a joke, a trick, a harmless prank.

Or if . . .

Someone pressed the front doorbell and kept it clanging.

Gretchen sucked in a deep shuddering breath and held it. Fighting back her panic, she forced her trembling legs forward. To the door. The bell deafening now.

She grabbed the knob in both hands and pulled with all her strength. The door shot open, sending her tumbling back, off-balance. She stared wide-eyed at the face in the doorway—and screamed. "Mom? It was *you*?"

Mrs. Page shifted the hooded cloak she wore. "Sorry. I forgot my keys." She stepped into the house. "What took you so long, Gretchen?"

"I . . ." Gretchen gaped at her, her whole body still tense and trembling. "Mom, you tapped at the window? You went around back?"

"Of course not," Mrs. Page said, letting the cloak fall off her shoulders, wrapping it in her arms, and carrying it to the coat closet. "Marci from work dropped me off and I rang the front bell."

"But, Mom—" Gretchen started.

Someone banged on the window. And pounded on the back door.

"Close the door," Mrs. Page said. "You're letting the cold air in."

Gretchen stepped back to the door and started to push it shut. But she stopped when something caught her eyes. She squinted into the yellow porchlight.

Something on the evergreen shrub at the side of the front stoop. She stepped out of the house. The wind ruffled her T-shirt and tossed back her hair.

She tugged the object off the bush. And raised it into the light.

A bandanna. A red-and-yellow bandanna. It had become caught in the pine needles.

Gretchen stared at the bandanna, wrapping it around her hand. Where had she seen it before?

On Devra Dalby?

12.

On Saturday, tryout day, Gretchen awoke at five thirty in the morning and couldn't get back to sleep. Her mind was spinning. She kept going through routines she already knew by heart, routines she had done a thousand times.

I don't want to overthink. My moves should all flow easily from muscle memory.

But images of Devra kept interrupting, breaking her early morning concentration. Devra's face turning pink, then red as Gretchen refused to cooperate. Her features going so tight on her face. Her words spit through gritted teeth.

Gretchen couldn't remember ever seeing that kind of anger on another person.

Maybe Coach Walker showed Devra my highlight reel. Maybe Devra saw that she isn't as good as me. Maybe she realizes she can't compete.

Gretchen waited till seven thirty to call Polly. "I've

never been so crazy tense in my life," she told her old friend. "I tried to eat a bowl of cornflakes for breakfast, and I couldn't choke them down."

She took a deep breath. "I'm tense, Polly, but I'm also totally psyched. Devra didn't ruin my confidence. I know I'm an outstanding cheerleader, and I know I can contribute to this squad. It's not like I want to prove anything to Devra. I only want to win this for myself. You understand, don't you?"

Gretchen did some stretching exercises in the backyard. It was a cool, gray morning with tiny raindrops in the air. Low overhead, a black storm cloud rolled closer, darkening the sky to near nighttime.

She turned and gazed at Madison's house next door, somehow expecting to see Madison practicing her violin in the window. But the house was dark.

Gretchen wanted to practice a few running cartwheels. But the rain started to come down harder, blown into her face by gusting winds. She trotted back into the house.

In her room, she pulled on a tank top and yoga pants. Swept her blonde hair straight and tied it tight with a plastic barrette. She checked herself out one last time in the mirror. "You can do this," she told her reflection.

She found the keys to her mother's Camry on the table in the front entryway, and was nearly to the front door when her mother appeared. "What's up, Gretchen?"

Gretchen frowned at her. "You know perfectly well what's up. I'm going to my cheerleader tryout. Are you going to wish me good luck?"

"Of course," her mother replied, apparently startled by Gretchen's sharpness. "Can I give you a hug?" She opened her arms.

Gretchen had no choice. She stepped forward, and they had a brief, awkward hug. Her mom wasn't the touchy-feely kind of person, and that was okay with Gretchen. At least, she had grown used to few hugs or kisses or almost no physical signs of affection from her mother.

"My mom isn't cold. She's just not very approachable," she'd told Polly once a year or so ago.

"Is that why your parents got divorced?" Polly had asked.

Gretchen shuddered. "Eww. I don't want to think about that."

The hug ended quickly, and Gretchen started to the door.

"I just want to say one thing," Mrs. Page said, blocking her path. "I know you have high hopes, dear. But if you don't get the position, you have to remember it isn't the end of the world."

Gretchen's mouth dropped open. "Excuse me?"

"I mean you're new in this school, and it might be nice to settle in. You know, get used to things and make new friends and get comfortable in your classes. If you don't make the team—"

"Mom, I don't *believe* you!" Gretchen snapped. "Why do you do this to me? Why are you always trying to discourage me and pull me down?"

Mrs. Page took a step back. She pressed a hand against her throat and gaped at Gretchen, as if hurt and surprised. "Pull you down? I would *never* do that, dear. I just don't want you to be crushed if you fail today."

"Fail? *Fail?*" Gretchen could feel herself losing it. She suddenly pictured a huge, red bomb about to explode.

"I never want to discourage you," her mother said. "But I don't think it's wise to get your hopes up. That's all."

Gretchen could feel the good energy flowing out of her. Her mother always knew exactly how to bring her down. With a cry of disgust, she bumped past her mother, burst out the door, and slammed it hard behind her.

I can nail this tryout, she told herself. *I know I can nail it.*

13.

Devra was already in the gym when Gretchen arrived. She was doing stretching exercises near the far wall. She wore a maroon-and-white Shadyside jersey over white Spandex shorts. Her red hair fell loosely around her face as she stretched.

Courtney, in her cheerleader uniform, stood with Devra, leaning against the wall. The two girls chatted easily. Neither one of them turned to greet Gretchen.

Stacy and the other cheerleaders were all in uniform—Ana, perky-looking with green cat eyes and short, straight black hair, bangs across her forehead; Becka, crinkly brown hair falling around a slender serious face, at least a head taller than Ana; and Shannon, tall and athletic, with cocoa-brown skin, round, dark eyes, her black hair pulled to one side in a tight ponytail.

They clustered around the doorway to Coach Walker's office. Through the glass office wall, Gretchen could see Walker talking on the phone.

One person sat in the bleachers at the back of the gym. As Gretchen crossed the floor, she recognized Sid. He waved to her, a can of Coke in his other hand.

Stacy turned to greet her. "Hey, Gretchen. This is exciting. Are you psyched?"

Gretchen swallowed, her mouth suddenly dry. "Well . . . that's *one* way to put it. Actually, I'm terrified."

"I get nervous, too," Stacy said. "I think it helps me perform better. You know. Gets the adrenaline going."

Coach Walker hung up the phone and stepped into the office doorway. She glanced around. "Are we all here?"

"Yes, we are," Stacy replied. "Ready to rock and roll."

Normally, Gretchen would hate Stacy's kind of rah-rah enthusiasm. But Stacy was the only cheerleader acting warm and welcoming to her. So she decided she had to like Stacy's bright personality.

I wish I could be more like her.

"Gretchen, did you bring any music or anything?" Coach Walker asked.

"No. I'm just going to do a basic routine and show some jumps and moves."

"Stacy and Ana will help you if you want to include any Thigh Stands or High Jumps," Coach Walker said. She motioned with her head toward Ana, who smiled at Gretchen.

"I think we'll let Devra go first," Walker said. She

70

turned and shouted: "Devra? Courtney? Would you like to join us? Are you ready to begin?"

Devra did a few more leg stretches, then followed Courtney toward the others. Her eyes were on Gretchen as she approached. She nodded but didn't say hello.

Devra took a towel from the shelf in the coach's office and mopped her forehead. "I think I'm warmed up." She picked up a bag that leaned against the wall, pulled out a water bottle, and took a long drink.

"Follow me, everyone," Coach Walker said, motioning with one hand. She led the way across the gym to the bleachers. Sid raised his Coke can in greeting as the cheerleaders took seats on the bottom benches. Gretchen was too nervous to sit down. She stood at the side of the bleachers, gripping the railing tightly.

"Devra, you're up," Coach Walker said. "Show us something, okay?"

Devra nodded, wiping water off her chin. She set down her water bottle. Then she brushed back her red hair and stepped to the middle of the floor. As she stepped into place, the sky outside brightened, the storm clouds parted, and yellow sunlight washed through the high windows of the gym.

"Great special effects, Devra," Coach Walker called. "You brought your own spotlight."

The cheerleaders leaned forward on the bleacher benches and grew silent, preparing to watch. Gretchen crossed her arms in front of her. She took a deep breath and held it. If only her heartbeats would stop fluttering like a hummingbird's wings.

She turned in time to see Sid flash her a thumbs-up.

"Go, Devra!" Courtney shouted.

Stacy scooted close to Gretchen. "Courtney and Devra have been friends forever," she whispered. "But don't worry. Courtney isn't going to vote. The other cheerleaders don't vote. Only Coach Walker and I will decide who wins."

Gretchen started to reply, but Devra had begun her tryout.

"I'm going to do a few new cheers that I wrote," she announced. "I've been practicing different jumps, and I'll show them to you. It's hard to stand here and do this alone. I think you all know that I'm a *team* player, and I do my best work when you others are with me. I think I need your support—"

"Can we skip the acceptance speech?" Coach Walker interrupted, raising one hand to signal for Devra to stop.

A few girls laughed. Ana whispered something to Shannon beside her.

"This isn't a joke, Coach Walker," Devra said, scowling. "You know I'm trying out under protest. Everyone knows I worked hard all last year and I deserve this spot on the squad."

Walker shook her head. "Devra, please. We all know how you feel. You're not exactly shy about telling people.

But we want what's best for the squad. We have a good chance of going to the state tournament this year. You know that. So we have to put the best team we can out there. You want that, too, don't you?"

Devra rolled her eyes and didn't answer.

An awkward silence fell over the gym. Devra gazed at Gretchen for a long moment, as if challenging her. Then she stepped into position and delivered one of the new cheers she had written.

"Do you dig it?
That Tiger beat!
Have you got it?
Stomp your feet!
Go, Tigers!"

Gretchen watched, still standing tensely with her arms crossed tightly over her chest, and felt some of her anxiety fade. *Devra isn't very good*, she realized. *Her Toe Touch Jumps were okay. But those are the simplest jumps in the world. Her Spread Eagle Jump at the end looked awkward, off-balance.*

Everyone watched in silence as Devra did a short and simple floor routine with some basic tumbling tricks. The sunlight washed down on her, making the floor shine and sending her shadow in all directions.

She isn't bad, Gretchen thought. *But she has no spark. And she keeps forgetting to smile. She's going through the routine, but she isn't selling it.*

"Here's another cheer I wrote," Devra announced.

She picked up a pair of red pom-poms from beside some water bottles beneath the lowest bench. Then she trotted back to her spot, turned, and performed her cheer.

"Do you dig it?
That Tiger beat?
Tigers roar!
More! We want more!
Tigers roar! Tigers SCORE!
GO, TIGERS! YAAAY!"

Devra punctuated each line with a tuck jump, raising both arms in a High V, then tucking her knees to her chest as she jumped. She finished with a series of Pike Jumps. Each time she jumped, she brought her legs up to meet her hands. She had good height on the pike, but her landing on the toe touch was off, and she struggled to keep her balance.

The girls clapped as Devra came running off the floor. A grin on her face, she shook the pom-poms above her head, as if in triumph.

She isn't terrible, Gretchen thought. *But she isn't very good, either. Especially if she had all last year to practice with the squad.*

Gretchen knew she was a better cheerleader. She knew this fact should help her lose her nervousness. But the heavy feeling in her stomach didn't fade, and her hands remained ice cold and sweaty.

Coach Walker looked up from her clipboard, where she had been rapidly scribbling notes about Devra's performance. "Good job, Devra," she said.

"I can do the Pike Jumps a lot better," Devra said. "I usually get my legs up higher at practice."

"It's not an easy jump," Walker said, writing some more on the clipboard pad. "I liked the cheers you wrote. The second one needs a little work on the cadence. But . . . very good."

"Thanks," Devra said. "I think they'll work for basketball, too."

"And air hockey!" Sid chimed in.

That made some of the girls laugh. Devra just glared at him.

Coach Walker shook her head. "Thanks for sharing that, Sid."

"Just trying to keep it light," Sid replied.

Devra took a seat next to Courtney. The two girls whispered together. Stacy leaned close to Gretchen and murmured, "Go out there and nail it!"

Gretchen stepped into the bright rectangle of sunlight on the gym floor. She took a deep breath and held it. To her surprise, she suddenly didn't feel so tense. She raised her arms in a V and practiced a straight Cheer Leader Jump. A grin spread over her face. She felt light and strong.

I can do this.

"Tigers roar!
Roar Tigers Roar!
Tigers roar!
Tigers SCORE!

She knew her Toe Touch Jumps were perfect. She performed the cheer again, this time with Spread Eagles. She showed off with a Double Hook Jump, kicking her legs out to the side, hooking her feet.

Time to REALLY show off!

Her running cartwheels made some of the girls gasp. Her Power Jumps were perfect. The double cartwheel into a Hook Jump made them burst into applause.

Gretchen ran off the floor, screaming, "Go, Tigers!" Cheering herself.

Coach Walker had her head down, writing on the clipboard pad. "Excellent job," she told Gretchen. "Very smooth and confident."

Stacy moved next to Coach Walker and said something in her ear. The coach nodded. Stacy gestured toward Gretchen and said some more to the coach.

Gretchen watched them intently. *Stacy and Coach Walker are the only two voting on who makes the team,* she thought. *What are they saying?*

Two rows up, Courtney was patting Devra's shoulder. Devra kept shaking her head, her eyes down. Courtney was obviously reassuring her.

Gretchen's heart was pounding. Sweat rolled down

her forehead. She grabbed a water bottle from under the bleachers and raised it to Devra. "Is this yours?"

Devra motioned with one hand. "Go ahead. Take it."

Gretchen mopped her forehead with her arm. Then she uncapped the bottle, tilted it to her mouth, and drank it nearly to the bottom.

Devra suddenly jumped to her feet. "Coach Walker, can I do some more? I didn't really show off my floor tumbling routine."

Coach Walker lowered her clipboard. "No. I think that should be enough," she told Devra. "You both did five minutes and showed us your best moves and—"

"No. I didn't show you my best moves," Devra insisted. "I thought you'd want to see my basic jumps. But I do much harder stuff." She frowned at Gretchen. "I don't do all those cartwheels. I mean, I'm not a circus clown. I don't see what they have to do with leading a crowd in cheers."

Coach Walker jumped to her feet, too. "That's enough, Devra. Let's keep this nice and civilized, okay?"

Devra didn't reply. She sat back down, shaking her head. Courtney leaned closer to commiserate with her.

Gretchen stood at the side of the bleachers. Stacy and the coach were gazing at Coach Walker's notes, going over them line by line. Gretchen saw Ana slide next to Sid. He put his arm around her shoulders and whispered something in her ear. Ana giggled and shoved his arm away.

Gretchen's stomach rumbled. She suddenly felt strange. A wave of nausea rolled up from her belly, tightened her throat. She tried to swallow, but her throat had tightened.

Another wave of nausea made her stomach churn. She tried to force the feeling down. She felt really sick. Felt her stomach rumble and tighten.

"Ohhhh." A moan escaped her throat. She tried to fight back the feeling, struggled to keep her lunch down. But her stomach gave a sharp, violent lurch.

She grabbed her sides, shut her eyes, leaned over—and spewed a tidal wave of green-yellow vomit onto the gym floor at her feet.

An ugly groan burst from deep inside her. And another gusher of vomit poured onto the floor.

Holding her stomach, Gretchen bent over grunting and groaning as violent spasms shook her body, and her stomach continued to heave up everything it held.

Over her groans, Gretchen heard the startled cries of the other girls. She held her breath, trying to stop the sick upheavals.

Raising her head, she saw Coach Walker pick up the nearly empty water bottle at Gretchen's feet. The coach raised the bottle and sniffed it. "Hey," she said. "This doesn't smell right. Someone put something in this water bottle."

Gretchen spit the last glob of vomit onto the floor. Stacy handed her a towel. She wiped her face with it. Her whole body shook. She swallowed, swallowed again and again, her mouth bitter and sour.

Coach Walker put an arm around Gretchen's shoulders. "Are you all right? Do you feel better?"

Gretchen nodded. Then raised her eyes to the bleachers—and caught the pleased smile on Devra's face.

14.

She poisoned me, Polly. I know she did." Gretchen adjusted the phone on her ear.

She had driven home, still fighting down her nausea. Her head pounded, throbbed in pain. She ran into the house, to her bathroom, brushed her teeth for five minutes, struggling to scrub the sour taste from her mouth.

Her mother wasn't home. She left a note saying she was having dinner with a new friend she had met at the hairdresser's.

Gretchen couldn't wait to call Polly and tell her about the tryout.

Polly was speechless with shock. "Devra put something in the water," Gretchen told her. "Coach Walker sniffed it. She said it smelled like cleaning fluid or something."

Gretchen felt her stomach churn. She took a deep breath, then let it out slowly.

"I saw the smile on Devra's face," Gretchen continued.

"She was so proud of herself. But guess what? She loses. She loses, Polly, because I won the tryout. She wasn't in the same league, and everyone saw it. Even her friend Courtney knew that I was better."

Gretchen rubbed her forehead. *If only this headache would give me a break and go away.* It felt like some creature was trying to burst out of her skull. She shut her eyes, but it didn't help.

"If I tell Mom that Devra tried to poison me, she'll call the police," Gretchen said. "But Devra will only deny she did it. Look, they're going to announce the winner of the tryout in a few days. Devra's going to be an alternate all year, and she'll have to stand on the sidelines and watch me perform. That's punishment enough, don't you agree?"

Before Polly could reply, the doorbell rang. Gretchen said goodbye, tossed the phone onto her bed, and hurried to the front door.

Through the peephole, she saw a boy standing on the front stoop, his face hidden behind a gray hoodie. "Who's there?"

"It's me."

Me?

She pulled the door open. "Sid? Hi. I didn't expect—"

"Gretchen, are you okay?" He pulled back his hood. His eyes searched hers. "I was worried. I—"

"I feel a lot better," she said.

She stepped aside for him to come into the house. But

instead he wrapped his arms around her waist, lowered his face to hers, and kissed her. The kiss lasted a long time. She gave herself to it. Let all other thoughts leave her mind.

Kissed him. Kissed him . . . then pushed him away. *Stacy*. The name flashed into her thoughts.

Her face felt hot. On fire. She could still taste his lips on hers. She grabbed his hand and pulled him into the living room. Most of their furniture hadn't arrived yet from Savanna Mills. She tugged him to the couch facing the fireplace. He pulled her down on top of him and they kissed again, another long, lingering kiss.

Again, she broke the kiss and pushed him away. Her heart fluttered in her chest. She felt a rush of emotion, suddenly realized how attracted she was to him.

Stacy. Stacy is his girlfriend. This isn't right.

But it feels right.

Sid tugged down his hoodie and sprawled back on the couch, tilting his head back, gazing up at the bronze ceiling fixture. "Wow," he murmured. "Wow."

She slid to the couch arm. "Did you really come to see if I was okay?"

He nodded. "Whoa. Devra. I don't *believe* her."

"Do we have to talk about her?" Gretchen said, playing with the end his hoodie sleeve.

"You should have heard her ranting after you left," Sid said. "She's really psycho."

"Huh? You really think she's crazy?"

"No. I just think she's a spoiled brat. No one has ever said no to her. Devra always gets what she wants."

"Not this time," Gretchen said. "This time, Devra loses and I win."

Sid smiled. Gretchen saw that he had two tiny dimples in his cheeks when he smiled. He reached for her and started to pull her to him.

But she resisted. "Can we talk about something?" she asked.

He frowned. "You want to *talk*?" He ran a finger tenderly along her cheek.

"What about Stacy?" Gretchen asked.

Sid let out a long sigh. He pulled himself up straight. "Stacy? Stacy is a long story."

"Well . . . aren't you two going together?"

"Forever," he said. "We've been together forever. Our parents were all best friends. When I was little Stacy's family lived right across the street from us. Stacy and I played together when we were two years old."

"Whoa," Gretchen murmured.

"Yeah. Whoa." He rolled his eyes. "It's like we've been together forever. We're even going to college together. We're going to Wisconsin. Our parents expect us to get married. *Everyone* in our families expect us to get married. It's like this great romantic story, only . . . only . . ."

"Only what?" Gretchen demanded.

Sid took a breath. He shrugged. "I like her a lot. Seriously. But I don't want to marry her. I've tried to break up with her."

"Really?" Gretchen studied his face, trying to determine if he was telling the truth.

"Yes, really. I've tried to explain a dozen times. Tried to say we should just be friends. But I can't get through to her. She doesn't think I'm serious. I mean, I guess she doesn't want to believe the truth, that I want to break up with her."

"Everyone thinks you're the perfect couple," Gretchen said.

"Everyone is wrong," Sid said, lowering his eyes. "Stacy keeps acting like everything is perfect between us. You know how gung-ho she is. She's a cheerleader even when she isn't being a cheerleader. But . . ." He shook his head sadly.

Gretchen leaned forward. She placed her hands on Sid's cheeks and pulled him close. She shut her eyes and kissed him.

The tryout . . . Sid . . . things are finally going my way.

He left about ten minutes later. He had to do some shopping for his mom.

Gretchen leaned back on the couch, waiting for her heartbeats to slow. The image of him kissing her, kissing her lingered in her mind.

She felt as if she were floating on air as she picked

herself up and made her way upstairs to her room. As she entered, a bell *ding* on her phone startled her out of her dreamy thoughts.

She picked her phone up from where she had tossed it on the bed. She gazed at a text message on the screen:

YOU COULD BREAK YOUR NECK

All in capital letters. From Devra?

A chill tightened the back of Gretchen's neck as she read the words again.

The phone *dinged* again. Another message appeared beneath the first one:

SOMETIMES CHEERLEADERS DIE

Gretchen stared at the words until they blurred. She squeezed the phone so hard, her hand ached.

Is Devra serious? Am I really in danger?

15.

Madison set her violin down on the coffee table. She rubbed her neck as she crossed her living room and took the phone from Gretchen. "You got these messages right after the tryout?"

Gretchen nodded. "Do you believe it? How *crazy* is this?"

Madison studied the screen. "Well . . . they are definitely from Devra. There's her name under the phone number at the top. Devra Dalby. She didn't try to disguise it or anything."

Gretchen shook her head. "I guess she wanted me to know the texts came from her."

"Wow." Madison handed the phone back to Gretchen. "She doesn't care what she does. She thinks she's just above us all. It's like the rules of decency don't apply to her."

Gretchen blinked. "Rules of decency? This is just plain psycho, Madison. What do I do?"

Madison rubbed the soreness from her neck. Gretchen saw that her hands were covered in rosin. "I've been practicing for two hours," she said. "I don't want to look like a jerk in front of the string quartet."

Gretchen tucked the phone into her bag. "You won't look like a jerk. You play beautifully."

"What if I break a string or something?" Madison's eyes grew wide. "Oh, I'm sorry. We were talking about you. Sorry to be so self-obsessed."

"It's okay," Gretchen said, perching on the edge of a brown leather armchair and swinging her bag onto her lap. "I just don't know whether I should ignore these threats. I mean, how serious could they be?"

Madison pressed her hands against the waist of her jeans. "You can't ignore them, Gretchen. You have to report them."

"No way. I can't go to the police."

Madison shook her head. "No, not the police. You have to show them to Coach Walker. She needs to know what Devra is doing to you."

Inside Gretchen's bag, a bell rang. The phone.

Gretchen fumbled in the bag until she found the phone. She raised it to her face and read it. "Another message," she told Madison. "From Devra."

GIVE ME A K-I-L-L

Madison squinted at it. Her mouth dropped open. "Oh my God. Gretchen, that's a *death threat*. You have to show it to Coach Walker. You don't have a choice."

Coach Walker stared at the messages on Gretchen's phone. She kept blinking as if trying to blink them away. Her face at first had shown surprise. but now she stared blankly, all the emotion drained from her features.

She blew out a breathy whistle. "Wheeew."

"I had to show it to you," Gretchen said, her voice just above a whisper.

They were in Walker's office. The door was closed. Walker sat stiffly in her desk chair, the glare off the phone reflecting her troubled face. She wore a long-sleeved Shadyside High T-shirt over white gym shorts. Gretchen stood close beside her.

Outside the window, Gretchen could see the cheerleaders practicing a cheer in the center of the gym floor. Their shouts were muffled by the window glass.

"I think Principal Hernandez has to see this," Coach Walker said. She set the phone down on her desktop. "This is not a small thing, Gretchen. This is very bad."

Gretchen nodded. She didn't know what to say.

Walker started to rise from her desk chair. "Maybe we should talk to Devra first," she said. She didn't wait for a reply from Gretchen. She pulled open the office door and shouted for Devra to come.

Courtney and Becka were helping Devra practice a Thigh Stand. Devra perched high on their thighs, caught her balance, and raised her arms above her head. Hearing the coach's call, she leaped to the floor and came running to the office, her red hair bouncing behind her.

Coach Walker ushered her inside and carefully closed the door.

Devra brushed back her hair with both hands. She tugged her white sleeveless T-shirt down over her black tights. She gave Gretchen a quick glance, then turned to the coach. "You wanted to see me?"

Coach Walker motioned for Devra to take the wooden chair against the wall. "Devra I want to ask you about some text messages," she said.

Devra wrinkled her face, as if confused. "Text messages?" She glanced at Gretchen again.

Gretchen stood with her arms crossed beside the coach's desk. She held herself tightly, trying to stop her whole body from trembling. She gritted her teeth and tried not to show any emotion at all.

Coach Walker lifted the phone off the desktop and pushed the screen into Devra's face. "Did you send these threatening messages to Gretchen?"

Devra squinted at them, moving her lips silently as she read the messages. She raised her eyes to Coach Walker. "No way. I didn't send those."

The coach held the phone in front of Devra, held it steadily in front of Devra's face. "Look at the top of the screen, Devra," she said in a whisper. "That's your phone number at the top."

"I swear I didn't send those messages," Devra said, her

face bright pink. "Someone took my phone. My phone has been missing."

Gretchen felt a chill run down her back. *What a good liar she is. Look at that innocent, wide-eyed expression on her face. If she didn't send the texts, why is she blushing?*

"After the tryout," Devra said. "The phone wasn't in my backpack. I think someone stole it."

"Someone on the squad?" Coach Walker demanded.

Devra shrugged. "I don't know. I just know my phone was gone. Ask Courtney. She'll tell you I'm telling the truth. She helped me look for the phone, but we never found it."

Devra turned her gaze on Gretchen and her features tightened in anger. "You can't accuse me. I didn't do it. Do you think I'm crazy? Do you really think I'd send you a death threat? That's sick."

Gretchen opened her mouth to speak, but no words came out.

"You're sick," Devra said. "Did you send those texts to yourself? Did you send them to make me look bad? To get me in trouble and out of your way?" Devra was red-faced, screaming now. "It won't work, sicko. Because I didn't send them. I didn't! I didn't!"

Gretchen glared back at her without speaking.

She's lying. It's obvious. She's totally lying.

16.

The next day, Stacy met Coach Walker at her office in the gym. "I think this is going to be a very short meeting," Stacy said. "We both know which girl is the better cheerleader. It isn't a real puzzler, is it?"

Stacy was surprised by the grim expression on the coach's face. "I'm afraid it isn't that easy, Stacy," she said, avoiding Stacy's gaze. "If it was just up to you and me . . ." Her voice trailed off.

Stacy turned when she heard footsteps thudding across the gym floor. She saw Sid striding quickly toward them. Sid gave her a quick wave as he poked his head into the office. "Is there practice today, Coach Walker? Should I get out any equipment?"

"I made the announcement yesterday, Sid. No practice today." Coach Walker couldn't hide her impatience. "Stacy and I are meeting about the tryout and who will make the squad."

Sid grinned. "Do I get a vote?"

Coach Walker made a shooing motion with one hand. "Go away."

"I can take a hint," Sid said.

Stacy grabbed his arm as he turned to leave. "See you later?"

"Sure." He shoved his hands into his jeans pockets and jogged out of the gym.

"Where were we?" Walker said. She checked her watch. "We have to go to Mr. Hernandez' office."

Stacy blinked. "Excuse me? He's meeting with us? About the tryout?"

Coach Walker nodded. "He instructed me not to make a decision about the cheerleader position until he had a chance to speak to me." She hesitated. "Actually, he didn't want you at the meeting. He said it wasn't anything for a student to hear."

Stacy blinked. "Really?"

"But I reminded him that you are the captain of the squad," Walker said, "and you have a vote. I insisted that you be there. He finally said okay, if you promise to keep it all confidential."

"Wow." Stacy didn't know what else to say.

"Maybe I shouldn't have told you all this," Walker said. "But I think it's important for the captain of the squad to know what's what."

Stacy swept her hand back through her hair. "This is totally weird."

"I know," Walker said. She clicked off her desk lamp

and stood up. "Come on. Hernandez gets cranky if you keep him waiting."

Principal Hernandez was a big man with a big rectangular head, topped with close-cropped salt-and-pepper hair. He wore thick black-framed glasses that made his gray eyes appear to bulge like frog eyes. A short goatee, more gray than black, framed his square chin.

Hernandez had been a football lineman in college, and he kept in shape, his gray suits tight, almost unable to contain his bulging shoulders. He looked like a hulking giant of a man, and with his bulging eyes, his expression always appeared menacing, sour. But Shadyside High students knew him to be gentle and soft-spoken. No one ever saw him raise his voice or shout in anger.

He greeted Stacy and Coach Walker at the door, a coffee mug in one hand. "Come in." His expression was solemn as he led them through the front reception area to his office in back.

Hernandez pushed the door closed and motioned for them to take the leather guest chairs that faced his desk, cluttered with papers and files. "How are you, Stacy?" he asked, dropping heavily into his desk chair. "I saw your parents at the Fall Carnival at Shadyside General last week."

Stacy spread her hands over the soft leather arms of the chair. "Yes. My mom is on the board of the hospital," she said.

"We had a nice talk, mostly about you," Hernandez said, shoving a stack of files to the edge of the desk.

"That's nice," Stacy said awkwardly.

All through the conversation, Hernandez hadn't smiled. His eyes went from Stacy to Coach Walker. He tilted back in his chair and raised a hand to scratch the top of his head.

"I'm afraid you may not like what I have to say," he told the coach

"About the cheerleading tryouts?" Coach Walker asked, shifting her weight in the chair.

Hernandez nodded.

"Is there a problem?" the coach asked.

Hernandez nodded again. He remained silent for a long moment. He appeared to be thinking of how to begin.

"I just got off the phone with Daniel Dalby," he said finally. "Devra's father." He paused, watching for Stacy or the coach to react.

But they both sat still, their faces expressionless.

Hernandez cleared his throat and leaned forward, his arms crossed on the desktop. "Perhaps you're not aware of this, but Daniel Dalby is the biggest contributor to the school's development fund every year. The Dalby family donates more than a third of our budget."

"Whew." Coach Walker blew out a whoosh of air. "Very generous."

"Very generous and very needed by us," Hernandez said. Behind his glasses, his eyes were wary. As if he expected trouble.

"Mr. Dalby has been on the phone with me more than once in the past week," he continued. "He wanted to tell me how important being on the cheerleader squad is to Devra's college plans."

Hernandez cleared his throat again. "Seems Devra is desperate to go to Princeton and thinks extra-curricular points from cheerleading will help sway the university to accept her."

"But Mr. Hernandez—" Coach Walker started to protest.

He raised a hand to silence her.

"I know you held a tryout last week between Devra and the new girl, Gretchen Page. Can you tell me your feelings about the tryout?"

"Gretchen was a lot better," Stacy said, her hands clasped tightly in her lap.

"I think Stacy and I agree that Gretchen is a far better performer and a much more skilled athlete than Devra," Coach Walker said.

Hernandez frowned. "I'm sorry to hear that," he said. He lowered his eyes to the desk, as if avoiding their stares. "Because I'm afraid I have to step in here. I promised Daniel Dalby that Devra will be chosen for the squad."

Stacy gasped. Coach Walker's mouth tightened in anger. "That isn't right," she said. "Gretchen is a hard worker and a talented cheerleader."

"She's really awesome," Stacy chimed in. "Gretchen could take us to the state finals. She really could."

Again, Hernandez raised his hand. "I'm really sorry. But I don't care if she's an Olympic gymnast. We have to give the spot to Devra. I hope you'll understand. The school cannot afford to lose one-third of our development money. We just can't."

Stacy's mouth hung open. She suddenly felt as if she couldn't breathe. This was so unfair . . . so wrong.

Coach Walker pulled herself more erect. She appeared to stiffen in her chair, her jaw clenched. She tugged at one ear. "Am I really hearing this correctly?" she said finally, her voice just above a whisper. "We're going to give this spot to Devra because her family is rich?"

"I hope you won't make a fuss about this, Violet," Hernandez said. "Don't think I feel good about it. Because I don't. But I have to do what's right for the school. Sometimes reality means you have to make a hard decision. And my decision stands."

He gazed from the coach to Stacy. "You've promised not to discuss this with anyone, am I right?"

Stacy nodded. "Yes."

Walker opened her mouth to say something—but stopped. Her eyes were on the office doorway. Stacy and Hernandez followed her gaze.

And saw the door open a little more than a crack—and Gretchen Page standing with her face poking through the opening.

"Gretchen!" Coach Walker cried. "How long have you been standing there?

17.

It's so unfair," Gretchen complained to Madison. "I just can't believe they did it to me."

"I can't, either," Madison replied, taking Gretchen's arm. "Do you want to drown your troubles with a Cinnabon? Or with some cheesecake from the Cheesecake Factory?"

They were wandering through the Division Street Mall because Madison thought it might help Gretchen if she got out of the house. Gretchen had been locked in her room, pouting and pacing the floor, muttering to herself and shaking her fists at the mirror.

"I didn't cry," she told Madison. "I was too angry to cry."

"No one would blame you if you cried," Madison said. "You were robbed, Gretchen. It was worse than robbery. It wasn't fair in any way."

"I-I don't know how I'm going to get over this," Gretchen stammered. "I-I worked so hard. It meant so much to me. I know I could take this squad to the state tournament. I just know it. And now . . ."

"And now, Cinnabon or cheesecake?" Madison said.

Gretchen chose cheesecake. They made their way into the restaurant. The hostess led them to a booth against the back wall and dropped enormous menus on the table.

"We don't need menus," Madison told her. "We just want to bury ourselves in tall mountains of cheesecake."

"Your server will be with you in a second," the hostess said. She poured ice water into the two glasses on the table.

Gretchen tilted the glass to her mouth and took a long drink. She brushed a strand of blonde hair off her forehead. "I promise I'm going to stop talking about this soon. Seriously."

"Go ahead and vent," Madison said. "What are friends for?"

"Everyone saw that I'm a better cheerleader than Devra," Gretchen said, spinning the water glass between her hands. "Everyone knows it."

"Well," Madison said, "won't she feel like a total fake performing with the other cheerleaders, knowing she had to buy the spot?"

Gretchen shrugged. "Who knows what Devra feels?"

Madison patted the back of Gretchen's hand. "At least, you'll practice with the squad. If someone gets hurt or can't make a game, you'll have your chance."

Gretchen didn't seem to hear Madison. Her eyes had a faraway look. "Devra was so mean . . . so vicious," she said. "Those horrible texts she sent. . . . Putting something awful in my water bottle so I'd throw up in front of everyone. What kind of person does that to someone?"

"A bad person?" Madison said. "I'm just guessing here."

Gretchen didn't laugh.

"Hey, I'm trying to get you to smile," Madison said. "What Hernandez did was horrible. But you'll still be with the squad. And look on the bright side. Maybe now that she has the spot on the squad, Devra will stop playing all those dirty tricks on you."

Gretchen had that faraway look again. She remained silent and still for a long moment. And then she murmured in a soft whisper: "I still have the knife."

Madison blinked. She leaned closer to Gretchen across the table. "Excuse me? What did you just say?"

"I still have the knife," Gretchen whispered. And then her eyes appeared to come back into focus. She stared uncertainly at Madison.

"What knife?" Madison demanded.

Gretchen shook her head. "Knife? Did I say something about a knife?"

"Are you okay?"

Gretchen forced a smile. "I was daydreaming. Really. I don't know why I said that. Just crazy, that's all. I don't have a knife. Only in my dreams. I guess I was remembering the dreams."

"Y-you . . . scared me," Madison stammered. "Your face got all weird and—"

Gretchen sighed. "Let's change the subject. How are you doing with your practice for the string quartet assembly?"

The two chatted through tall slices of cherry cheesecake and Rocky Road cheesecake. At times, their talk was awkward with long silences. Gretchen tried, but she just couldn't pull herself out of her thoughts about Devra and the cheerleaders.

As Madison talked about fall term exams, Gretchen found herself thinking about Sid. Aside from her new friendship with Madison, Sid was one of the few bright spots in her new life in Shadyside.

She thought about how he wrapped her in his arms on the couch in her living room . . . how understanding he was . . . how thoughtful, and how he kissed her with such feeling . . . long, urgent kisses.

Gretchen didn't blame Stacy for wanting to hold onto him. But Sid assured Gretchen he was trying to get through to Stacy, trying to convince her that he was serious about ending things.

And then it will be Sid and me.

Gretchen knew if she could just keep her thoughts on Sid, she would feel a lot better . . . concentrate on the positive. But it was so difficult.

And then there he was.

"Oh, wow." Gretchen gazed to the front of the restaurant and saw the hostess leading a tall boy in a denim jacket and black straight-legged jeans to a table. The boy had his hand on the waist of a girl with long black curls down past the shoulders of her blue sleeveless top.

It took only a few seconds to recognize Sid.

Gretchen stared at the hand he had on the girl's waist, guiding her to the table.

Madison caught Gretchen's stare. "Hey, what's wrong?"

"It's Sid," Gretchen said. "And he's with another girl." She slid to the edge of the seat and jumped up from the booth.

"Gretchen?" Madison called. "Hey, Gretchen. Where are you going? Come back here. What are you doing?"

18.

Gretchen heard her friend shouting after her, but she didn't turn around. Her heart pounding, the cheesecake suddenly making her stomach feel heavy as lead, she stomped through the narrow aisle toward the table. Sid was just sitting down. The girl already had her menu raised in front of her.

Too much bad news, Gretchen found herself thinking. *First I'm cheated out of my cheerleader spot. Then . . .*

She took a deep breath. She wanted to act calm, nonchalant in front of Sid and this girl. She didn't want to act like a crazy person. After all, she and Sid didn't really have any kind of understanding.

He had indicated in every way that he was dumping Stacy for her. Gretchen hadn't imagined that. She wasn't jumping to conclusions. The way he kissed her that day . . .

She strode up to the table and gripped the back of the

empty chair with both hands. "Hey, Sid—" She felt pleased that her voice didn't tremble.

The girl had big, dark blue eyes. They grew wide as she returned Gretchen's gaze. Her hair was beautiful, Gretchen thought. Long strands of of shiny black curls that caught the light from overhead and glistened like starlight.

Sid didn't show any surprise. "Gretchen, hi. How's it going? Are you feeling any better about the cheerleader thing?"

"Not really," she replied. He didn't seem eager to introduce her to this new girl. She motioned with her eyes, thinking maybe he'd take the hint.

"Oh, yeah," he said, setting down the tall menu. "This is my cousin Maya."

His cousin?

They *did* have the same dark hair. They were both tall and thin.

"Maya lives in Martinsville," Sid explained. "We don't get to hang out that often."

His cousin.

Gretchen suddenly felt a lot lighter. "Nice to meet you," she said, forcing a smile.

Sid motioned to the empty chair. "Want to join us?"

"Oh. No. I can't," Gretchen said. "I'm here with Madison." She pointed.

"Well, okay. See you," Sid said.

"Nice to meet you," Gretchen said to Maya. Had she already said that? She turned and made her way back to Madison.

Behind her, she heard Maya ask Sid, "Who was that?"

A baby started crying at the table beside her and drowned out Sid's reply.

"It's his cousin," she told Madison, sliding back into the booth.

"Really?"

"I think so," Gretchen said. "I don't think he'd lie to me."

"Don't get ahead of yourself with Sid," Madison said.

"Excuse me? What does *that* mean?"

"It means don't get ahead of yourself with Sid."

The text message came after school the next afternoon. Gretchen wondered why no one had mentioned a special meeting to her during the day.

She read the message twice to make sure she had it right:

Hey, it's me Stacy
Important squad meeting.
Cheerleaders & alternate.
8 2night in the gym.
Don't be late.
Go, Tigers

At dinner, her mother argued with her. "Do you

really think you should give up your homework time for a meeting so late at night? Shouldn't you be using your time better? You're not even on the squad."

Gretchen set down her fork. "How many times are you going to remind me, Mom?"

"I'm just saying . . ." Mrs. Page hesitated. "I'm just saying don't let the cheerleading thing take over your life. They didn't want you on the squad and—"

Gretchen raised her hand. "Stop. Just stop. You're just going to start a screaming fight, Mom. Between the two of us. I showed you the message. Stacy said cheerleaders and alternate. That's me. So I'm going tonight. That's it."

Her mother opened her mouth to reply, but thought better of it. "Whatever," she muttered and returned to her tuna and macaroni casserole.

Gretchen pulled her mother's car into the student parking lot a little before eight. Two other cars were parked near the teachers' lot. Two spaces down, a squirrel sat straight up, rolling an acorn between its paws. It turned and scampered away as Gretchen opened her car door to climb out.

Her sneakers thudded loudly in the long, empty hall. Someone had left their locker door open, and papers and notebooks had spilled out onto the floor. Gretchen hummed to herself, and her voice rang hollow against the tile walls.

Stepping through the double doors, she blinked against the bright light of the gym. All of the lights had been turned on, and the gym floor glowed like a yellow sun, reflecting the lights.

"Anyone here?" Her eyes swept from the bleachers against the far wall, across the empty floor, to the glass-windowed offices at the side. "Hey? Anyone?" Her shout echoed all around her.

She pulled out her phone and glanced at the time. 8:05. She checked to see if she had received any other texts. No.

"Where is everybody?" she asked out loud.

Gretchen moved to Coach Walker's office and leaned back against the closed door. She checked her Snapchat and her email, but kept raising her eyes to the gym entrance, expecting to see the others arrive.

At 8:15, she began to suspect that something was wrong. Pacing back and forth along the wall now, she retrieved Stacy's text message. She read it again. Then she tried to reply:

I'm at the gym.

Where is everybody?

Did I get the night wrong?

She pushed *send*, but the message wouldn't go. She pressed *send* again.

And gasped when all the lights went off.

"Hey—!" The deep darkness hit her like an ocean wave. She actually stumbled back against the wall. "Hey—!" She frantically tried to blink away her blindness. But it had been so bright, and now . . .

"Hey, somebody! Who turned off the lights?" Her voice revealed her surprise.

The narrow windows along the top of the walls were solid black. Gretchen turned toward the doors. The windows in the gym doors were black, too. Someone had turned off the hall lights.

Gretchen took a deep breath and fought back her fear. *Are the school lights on a timer? Or did someone deliberately turn them off?*

"Hey, anyone?" she shouted again. "I'm in here. Turn the lights back on."

No reply.

Silence.

Then she heard a loud *click*. From the entrance doors?

"Hey—is someone there? *Answer* me!"

Silence.

And then a soft footstep. And a cough. And another soft scrape of a shoe against the floor.

"Who is it?" Her voice suddenly tiny, trembling. "Who's there? I hear you."

I've got to get out of here.

Her back against the wall, Gretchen began edging toward the doors. The blackness pulsed before her eyes. She couldn't see anything.

But she knew she wasn't alone.

More scraping footsteps. And then Gretchen heard the shallow breathing of someone close by.

She sucked in another breath. And the scent invaded

her nose. A sweet citrus scent. It took a few seconds to recognize it. The citrus scent Devra used.

"Oh, wow," she murmured. "Devra? Is that you?"

She didn't wait for an answer. She grabbed the bar on the gym door and shoved it hard.

It didn't budge.

She pushed the door. Leaned into the next door and pushed it.

No. Locked.

That was the clicking sound. Devra had locked it. Turned off the lights and locked the doors. Locked her in. And now was moving slowly toward her.

If only she could see in this thick blackness. . . .

"Devra, I know it's you. Devra, you're not scaring me. SAY something!"

Silence.

"Devra—you've already WON! Why are you doing this to me?"

Another muffled cough in reply. And then . . . running footsteps.

Gretchen squinted into the darkness. She froze. She didn't know which way to run. Panic paralyzed her as her pursuer came at her hard, footsteps thudding loudly in the dark, empty gym.

And then Gretchen opened her mouth in a scream as a body crashed into her, bone-hard shoulder diving into her middle, taking her breath away, slamming her to the floor.

19.

Unable to breathe, pain like a fire in her stomach, Gretchen hit the floor hard. She rolled onto her side and curled up to protect herself. Choking, struggling to get her breath back. It felt as if heavy black waves were rolling over her, pressing her down.

Was Devra going to keep fighting? Was she done hurting her?

Still gasping, Gretchen looked up when she heard the gym doors open and then slam shut. She heard the footsteps of her attacker out in the hall.

Forcing herself to breathe, she sat up. She gazed into the swirling darkness, waiting for the pain to fade, waiting for her chest to stop burning, for her head to clear.

Devra, I know it was you.

You shouldn't have worn that perfume, Devra.

She knew her attacker. But what good did that do? If she accused her, Devra would just deny it. Gretchen had no proof. In the thick darkness, she hadn't even seen Devra.

I have to wait. I have to stay on guard and wait my turn.

I'll find a way to stop her from terrorizing me.

I know my turn will come.

"We have to talk about fire batons," Stacy said.

After school on Wednesday found them heading to the gym for practice. With the first Tigers football game Friday night, the practices were becoming more intense. Gretchen was pleased that Coach Walker allowed her to practice some of the routines, even though she wouldn't be cheering with the squad Friday night.

Gretchen put a hand on Stacy's arm to stop her. "Can I ask you a question first?"

Stacy nodded. "Sure."

Gretchen pulled out her phone. "Did you send me this text message?" She showed her the message that brought her to the gym.

Stacy's eyes went wide. "No way," she said. "Someone used my name? There *was* no practice last night, Gretchen."

Gretchen tucked the phone back into her bag. "That's what I thought."

"Well, what happened?" Stacy demanded. "You didn't go to the gym, did you?"

"Of course not," Gretchen lied. "I knew it was a phony."

"What a dumb joke," Stacy said, shaking her head.

"Yeah. Dumb," Gretchen said. "So . . . tell me about fire batons. We didn't have fire batons at my old school."

"Well, we do a fire baton routine at halftime," Stacy said. "Lighting them is a little tricky. And since it's your job as the alternate to light them, I thought I should give you a lesson."

"I light them?" This assignment caught Gretchen by surprise. "I light them and hand them to a cheerleader?"

Stacy nodded. "Yes. Didn't Coach Walker talk to you? She probably forgot. No problem. I'll show you."

Coach Walker greeted them both. "I'm going to give Gretchen a fire baton tutorial," Stacy said.

The coach called Sid over. He had been sitting on the bottom bleacher, sharing a sandwich with Ana. "Sid, set up the kerosene bucket and bring out a couple of fire batons. Stacy and Gretchen are going to practice outside."

"No problem," Sid said, giving the coach a two-fingered salute. He grinned at Gretchen. "Lesson Number One. Don't burn down the school if you can help it."

"That's very helpful, Sid," Coach Walker said. "But we really don't want to hear Lesson Number Two. Just go get the equipment."

A few minutes later, Stacy and Gretchen stood in the grassy area behind the gym. It was a warm fall day. High clouds floated over the yellow and red leaves of the trees. A fat crow peered down at them from the low roof of the building, cawing angrily as if telling them to go away.

Sid set two blue plastic buckets in front of them. One was half-filled with kerosene, the other with water. He handed two fire batons to Stacy. And he pulled a couple of heavy rags from his jeans pocket.

Stacy stepped forward and gave him a quick kiss. "See you later?"

Sid's face reddened. He glanced at Gretchen. "Yeah. Maybe." He started back into the gym, but turned at the door. "Hey. Almost forgot." He pulled something from his shirt pocket and tossed it to Gretchen. A large candle lighter. "Have fun." He disappeared into the gym.

"It's very simple. Watch," Stacy said. She demonstrated as she talked. "They look like normal batons, but they have these big bulbs on the end that catch fire. Here's all you do. You dip one end of the baton into the kerosene. Then you dip the other end. Then you use the rag and wipe it off carefully to make sure no kerosene dripped onto the baton part. We don't want flaming cheerleaders, do we?"

Gretchen laughed. "That could be an awesome finale."

Why am I making jokes? Gretchen thought. *This is more dangerous than I thought.*

"Then you hold the baton sideways like this and light one end, then the other." She clicked the lighter. It flamed and Stacy held the flame over each end of the baton. "You hand one to Devra, then light another one and hand it to me," she instructed. "Easy?"

"Ha," Gretchen said. "Not so easy. But I think I can do it. Let me try one."

Stacy handed her the other baton. Gretchen twirled it in one hand, let it fly high in the sky, and caught it as it dropped. "Can you believe I took twirling lessons in third grade?"

"You are so talented," Stacy said, her voice light. She doused her fire baton in the water bucket Sid had brought out. She leaned close to Gretchen. "Listen, I feel bad about what happened. You know. You really are talented. What they did wasn't right."

"Thanks for saying that," Gretchen said. She turned and dipped one end of her baton into the kerosene bucket. She suddenly felt confused. She liked Stacy. Stacy was a nice person. But she didn't want to get too friendly with her. After all, she was stealing Stacy's boyfriend.

How could they possibly be friends?

"Dip it quickly," Stacy instructed. "You don't want to soak it."

Gretchen flipped the baton and dipped the other end. Then she grabbed a rag from Stacy and carefully wiped the middle of the baton. When she was sure it was dry, she lighted both ends. "Should I try to twirl it?"

"Better not. It takes a lot of practice. You have to hold it pretty far away from you."

"I want to try," Gretchen said. "If I catch fire—"

She didn't finish her sentence. The gym door swung open and Coach Walker stuck her head out. "What are you doing? Are you roasting marshmallows out here?" she called.

"Just teaching Gretchen the basics for Friday night," Stacy said.

"Come in," the coach said, waving them in. "I have a surprise for everyone."

Gretchen doused her baton in the water bucket. Then she tossed it on the ground and followed Stacy back into the gym.

She saw Sid standing in the center floor beside a pile of boxes.

"The new uniforms have arrived," Coach Walker announced. "Sid, hand them out. Come on, everyone. Go try them on."

A lot of excitement, cheers, and eager talk. Sid raised the boxes and called out the names. "Devra . . . Courtney . . . Shannon . . . Becka . . . Ana. Gretchen held her breath. Would there be a new uniform for the alternate?

Yes. Her box was at the bottom of the stack. Sid handed it to her, and she trotted to the locker room to try it on. The girls had strewn the boxes all over the locker room floor. Gretchen pulled hers from the box. A short, pleated maroon skirt with a long-sleeve maroon sweater top, a large white S on the front, a growling full-color tiger on the right shoulder.

Sweet.

The skirt fit perfectly. She kept turning it, trying to

find the front. It didn't seem to matter. She pulled on the top and adjusted it over the skirt. Tugged down the sleeves.

Sweeping back her hair with both hands, Gretchen turned to Ana at the locker across from her. "What do you think?"

"Lookin' good," Ana said. "These new uniforms are a lot hotter than the old ones." She bounced off to look at herself in the mirror beside the shower room door.

Arms around each other's shoulders, Courtney and Devra were performing a cheer together between the lockers. Gretchen adjusted the sleeves again. The sweater felt a little tight. No. Not tight. A little stiff. She stretched her arms out.

Her back started to itch. She tried to scratch it but couldn't reach. The uncomfortable feeling spread to her shoulders. Her stomach began to itch.

What's happening?

She rubbed her arms, scratched her shoulders. Her whole body prickled.

Something was wrong. Gretchen stumbled to the mirror. The backs of her hands itched now. Her chest felt aflame.

"What on earth—" she murmured, scratching her itching neck.

She stepped up close to the mirror, squinted hard, studying herself—and opened her mouth in a horrified scream.

20.

C ourtney and Devra stopped their cheer. The locker room grew silent.

A hand gripped Gretchen's shoulder. She spun around to see Stacy holding onto her, her eyes wide with surprise. "Gretchen? What's wrong?"

"Look! Look!" Gretchen cried. "Look at them. Cockroaches. Don't you see them? My uniform. It's *crawling* with cockroaches."

Stacy stepped back, her dark eyes bulged in horror. "I see them. Oh, yuck. Hundreds."

"They—they're crawling on my skin!" Gretchen cried. "Crawling all over me. Like little pinpricks. Oh, help." She started slapping at herself, slapping her sides, her chest. "Help. Get me out of this!"

The other girls clustered around her, eyes wide in shock. Stacy stared at her, helpless, open-mouthed. "The other uniforms are perfectly fine."

Two orange-brown cockroaches slithered up Gretchen's

neck. A few had climbed into her hair. She scraped both hands over her head, twisting, squirming. She rubbed her back against the wall. Cockroaches fell at her feet and scampered across the concrete floor.

Becka and Ana screamed and backed away. Shannon covered her mouth with both hands.

"Ohhhhhh." A sick groan escaped Gretchen's throat. Then, suddenly, her expression changed. Her face reddened and she clenched her jaw, narrowing her eyes, as if she was pondering a new idea.

Then, with an angry cry, she hurtled forward and grabbed Devra by the shoulders and spun her around. "YOU did this!" she screamed. "YOU did it! I know you did it!"

Devra pulled out of Gretchen's grip and stepped away from her, eyes wide with surprise. "Let *go* of me. Are you crazy? What are you talking about?"

"Look! Look what Devra did!" Gretchen cried, turning to confront everyone. She tugged the front of her sweater. Eight or ten cockroaches tumbled to the floor.

Gretchen pulled a cockroach off her neck and tossed it at Devra. It slid off Devra's sleeve and dropped to her feet.

"How could you *do* this to me?" Gretchen screeched in a high voice she had never heard before. "You won. You won, okay? I lost. So why are you torturing me?"

Coach Walker burst into the locker room. She stepped

into the circle of cheerleaders and took Gretchen by the shoulders. "Take a breath, Gretchen. Take a deep breath. Let's take this uniform off you. Then you can take a nice long shower."

"Why does she always blame me?" Devra cried. "Why does she blame me for everything?"

"Because you did it?" Gretchen said in a trembling voice. She moved toward Devra as if to fight her.

"You're totally psycho," Devra said. "Seriously. You're crazy. Why would I do that? Where would I get all those cockroaches?"

Gretchen brushed cockroaches off her legs and frantically tried to stomp on them. "Everyone knows you've declared war on me," Gretchen said through gritted teeth. "Everyone."

Devra crossed her arms over her chest. Her blue eyes were cold as ice as she returned Gretchen's stare. "I don't care about you," she said. "I never even *think* about you. So why should I go to the trouble of filling your uniform with bugs?"

"Because you know I'm better than you!" Gretchen shrieked. "You know I'm a better cheerleader. You're a *fraud*, a fake, and you know it."

Devra rolled her eyes and frowned. She turned to Coach Walker. "She's crazy. Look at her. She's practically frothing at the mouth."

"Gretchen, we have to get you out of that uniform,"

Coach Walker said softly. "Let's get you into the shower. We're going to have to call an exterminator for the locker room now."

But Gretchen didn't move. "You don't believe me? You all think I'm crazy?"

No one said a word. Devra kept her cold stare on Gretchen.

"I know how to prove it," Gretchen said. "I know how to show you that Devra did this." She shook her head hard. Three or four cockroaches came tumbling out.

Coach Walker tugged her arm. "Come on, Gretchen. Let's—"

"No!" Gretchen cried. "Where did these uniforms come from, Coach Walker? Where did you order them from?"

Coach Walker shrugged. "I don't remember. I think . . ." Her voice trailed off.

"Let's check one of the boxes," Gretchen said.

Coach Walker bent down and picked up a box.

"Where did it come from?" Gretchen repeated. "Where do the uniforms come from?"

The coach pulled off the box lid. She pulled out a slip of paper. She slowly raised her eyes to Gretchen. "They come from Dalby's Department Store."

21.

Gretchen took a shower in the locker room, then took another long, hot shower as soon as she got home. But she couldn't stop her skin and her hair from itching. Thinking about the cockroaches crawling all over her head and body sent chill after chill down her back.

How could she stop thinking about it?

The uniforms came from Dalby's. That proved that Devra had to be the culprit. But Coach Walker wasn't about to accuse Devra or investigate in any way. And Gretchen knew that Principal Hernandez wouldn't do anything, either.

The Dalbys' money was too important to Shadyside High. Devra could do whatever she wanted and no one would ever make a move to stop her or punish her.

And, of course, the question that kept preying on Gretchen's mind was: *Just how far will Devra go? How dangerous is she?*

Gretchen paced back and forth in her room. She

rubbed her arms. She could still feel the cockroaches prickling her skin. She had her wet hair wrapped in a towel, and her hair at least had stopped itching.

Maybe I should wrap my whole body in towels. Make a nice cocoon to hide in.

Finally, she decided she needed to talk to Polly back in Savanna Mills. That might distract her, take her mind off her itching skin. She decided not to tell Polly about the cockroaches. It would only worry her and gross her out, and she would feel sorry for Gretchen.

Gretchen felt sorry for herself, but she didn't want anyone else to feel that way.

She'd always been a winner back in Savanna Mills— at least until the trouble started. She wanted everyone back home to think of her as a winner now.

Gretchen stretched out on her bedspread and rested her head on the headboard. It felt good to lie down. She could feel the anger and the anxiety floating off her. She shut her eyes and just breathed for a while, taking slow, steady breaths.

Then she punched Polly's number into the phone. Polly answered after the first ring. Somehow, she always answered after only one ring.

"How's cheerleading?" Gretchen asked after they greeted one another. "Do they miss me?"

"No way. They have *me*," Polly joked.

Polly had always been the only one who could compete with Gretchen. She was tiny, at least a head shorter than Gretchen, and energetic as if she had a powerful electrical current running through her. She was so light, she could jump higher than anyone. Her jumps and moves were so effortless, Gretchen accused her of being weightless.

"I miss you *so much*," Gretchen blurted out without intending. And to Gretchen's surprise, she had tears in her eyes. "Hold on a minute, Polly," she said. She lowered the phone and took a few deep breaths to get herself together.

All of the disappointment, anxiety, and anger in her new school had obviously gotten to Gretchen. She was more tense than she knew, and she felt as if her emotions were all tingling just beneath her skin.

"I'm totally psyched for the first game of the season on Friday," she told Polly. It wasn't entirely a lie. "You won't guess what my assignment is."

"Sit on the bench and watch the other girls perform?" Polly said.

"Ha-ha. You're so funny. Remind me to laugh."

"Sorry. I couldn't resist. I can't believe you're an alternate, Gretchen. You were the *best*."

"Anyway, my job is to light the fire batons. We never had fire batons. I think everyone thought they were too dangerous. Or maybe the school was just too cheap to buy them."

"We were lucky to have pom-poms," Polly said. "Remember? They were shedding all over the place?"

"I'm a little freaked about the fire batons," Gretchen confessed. "I mean the kerosene really flames up when you light it. I have to be really careful. I mean, what if I mess up and . . ." She didn't finish her sentence.

Her mother burst into the room.

Gretchen said a quick goodbye and ended the call.

"Hey, Mom—" Gretchen started. She sat up and fiddled with the towel around her hair.

Her mother picked up a T-shirt from the floor and started to fold it. "You took a shower?"

"Yeah. I . . . uh . . . felt grimy from practice," Gretchen said.

"Did you use my bath gel? It's almost out."

"No. I used soap. Why do you always accuse me of using your stuff?"

"Because you do?" She set down the T-shirt on top of the dresser and began to straighten some books on Gretchen's bookshelf. "Practice was so hard, you had to lie down in bed?"

"I'm just relaxing, Mom. At least, I was until *you* came in."

"Can't you ever be civil to me? I'm not allowed to spend any time with you?"

"Sorry." Gretchen stood up and removed the towel. She walked to the dresser mirror to brush out her hair, which was still damp. She turned. "Mom, please don't rearrange my room."

Mrs. Page shrugged. "Just trying to be helpful."

"It isn't helpful," Gretchen snapped. "It's annoying. You wouldn't like it if I went into your bedroom and started pawing over everything."

Her mother's cheeks reddened. "I wasn't pawing." She sighed. "Can't we have one conversation without snapping at each other's throats?"

Gretchen rolled her eyes. "Very dramatic, Mom." She gave her head a shake and her blonde hair fell into place. She set down the hairbrush and adjusted her top over her jeans. "I'm going out."

Her mother studied her. She brushed a strand of hair back from Gretchen's forehead. "Where?"

"A cheerleader meeting," Gretchen lied. She didn't care where she went. She didn't want to stay here with her mother. It wasn't just anger at her mother's attitude. Gretchen was afraid she might break down and tell the horrible things that were happening to her because of Devra.

Gretchen knew if she started to tell everything to her mother, the tears would start to flow. And Gretchen *never* wanted to cry in front of her.

When Gretchen cried, Mrs. Page was seldom sympathetic. She would freeze up. Clamp her teeth shut in a hard expression. Like putting up a wall in front of her face.

Gretchen's tears brought out a coldness in her mother that Gretchen never wanted to see. Better to keep things inside. Her relationship with her mother was hard enough without adding more emotion.

"You know, I've been thinking," Mrs. Page said, following Gretchen out the bedroom door and down the hall.

Uh oh, Gretchen thought.

"I think maybe being an alternate is a good thing for you, dear. It will give you time to adjust."

Gretchen exploded in a roar of curses.

"Language, dear," her mother said softly. "Please— watch your language."

Gretchen sucked in a deep breath. She waited for some of her anger to cool. "Mom, why do you say those things? You knew that would make me furious. You knew how disappointed I was. Why do you want to bring it up now and make it worse?"

Mrs. Page's eyes widened in shock. She placed an open hand at her chest, as if she had been punched. "I didn't mean—"

Gretchen stormed out the door. She could feel the blood pulsing angrily at her temples. *Why do I let her get to me like that? Why can't I ever just ignore the horrible things she says?*

She realized she had left the house without any idea of where she was going.

Maybe I'll take a long, aimless walk. Maybe I should get the car keys . . . .

She heard violin music from Madison's open window next door. Without thinking about it, she turned, walked across the lawn, and rang the bell at Madison's front door.

Madison greeted her warmly. "Hi. Come in. I needed an excuse to take a break." She led Gretchen into her bedroom and picked up the violin. "Listen to this. This is the most difficult section. I think I've almost got it."

Gretchen perched on the edge of Madison's pale blue bedspread and listened. The notes came fast and furious. Gretchen stared at Madison's fingers on the fingerboard, sliding so rapidly, Gretchen could barely see the movement.

"Awesome!" she declared when Madison finished. "It's . . . beautiful."

Madison laughed. "Aw, shucks. It was nothing." Then she added, "Just three days of practicing that one part."

Madison carefully slid the violin into its case. "What's up?"

Gretchen sighed. "More of the same. You really won't believe this."

Madison's expression grew serious. "Try me."

She told Madison about the cockroaches in the new cheerleader uniform.

"You're right. I don't believe it," Madison said, shaking her head. "It doesn't make sense, Gretchen. Devra knows she's won. She has the spot on the squad."

"I know," Gretchen agreed. "There's no reason for her to keep torturing me." She frowned. "Okay, okay. I know Devra doesn't like me. But there's no reason why—"

"I know some things about Devra," Madison interrupted. She lowered her voice to a whisper. "Seriously. I know some things about her."

"Like what?" Gretchen demanded.

Madison smiled, but she didn't answer.

22.

"Go, Tigers
Down the field!
Go, Tigers
We never yield!

Go, Tigers
We want more!
Go, Tigers
Score, score, SCORE!"

Gretchen tried hard to enjoy the game. But she couldn't hold back her feelings of frustration as she watched the other girls perform their cheers from the end of the bench on the sidelines.

She tried not to concentrate on Devra, who was the klutziest of all the girls and nearly dropped Becka during a simple Thigh Stand. But she couldn't help catching the smirk on Devra's face when she glimpsed Gretchen slumped on the bench by herself.

It had rained during the day. The field was wet and a heavy dampness clung in the chilly night air. The stands in the Tigers' stadium were nearly full, and the shouts and cheers were enthusiastic, partly because it was the first game of the season, and partly because the Tigers were mauling the visiting Yellow Jackets from Pleasant Springs. It was nearing halftime, and the Tigers were up 17–3 and threatening to score another touchdown.

"Tigers roar
More more more!
Tigers Roar
More more MORE!"

Gretchen mouthed the words along with the cheerleaders. She had to fight down the urge to leap up from her lonely spot on the sideline and perform the cheers on her own.

A renegade cheerleader. The thought made her smile.

A tap on her shoulder made her jump. She turned to see Sid, motioning to her eagerly. "See the clock?" he pointed. "Two minutes till halftime. I set up the kerosene and the batons over here."

She let him pull her to her feet. She thought he was about to kiss her, but he turned his face away quickly.

Stacy might be watching.

Had he told her the truth about breaking up with Stacy?

No time to think about that.

A roar went up from the stands as Cory Wagner, the Tigers' tailback, crushed through the Yellow Jackets' line into the end zone. Gretchen didn't see the touchdown. She was inspecting the kerosene bucket, then unfolding a rag to keep handy for wiping the baton down.

Her heartbeats began to race. She felt happy to be off the bench and contributing to the squad. Actually *doing* something. She picked up one of the batons and twirled it in front of her.

"Devra, then Stacy," she murmured to herself.

The plan was for Devra to take the first fire baton, Stacy the second. Then the two of them would run in front of the stands together and do their fiery routine side by side.

Gretchen's throat tightened as the teams ran off the field for halftime. The Tigers band began to play. Gretchen glanced up at the crowd. Many were standing and stretching. The aisles were filled with people heading down to the hotdog booth in the student parking lot.

As soon as the band finished its two numbers, it was time for the cheerleaders' halftime routines. Gretchen silently went over her instructions one more time. She held the first fire baton tightly, preparing to dip one end, then the other into the kerosene bucket.

Maybe I should test the lighter, she thought. But then she saw Coach Walker waving to her from the cheerleaders' bench. Gretchen set the baton down on the grass and trotted over to her.

"Is anything wrong?"

Coach Walker shook her head. "I just wondered if you are ready, Gretchen. Are you sure you're okay with this? Do you need Sid or anyone to help?" She had to shout over the blare of the band.

Gretchen shook her head. "I'm fine, Coach Walker. I'm on it!"

Coach Walker flashed her a thumbs-up. Gretchen turned and trotted back to the fire batons.

A light cheer went up as the band finished its second song. The stands rang with laughter and shouts, people talking to friends, standing in small groups, gulping hotdogs and sodas.

"Show time," Gretchen murmured. "Here we go."

She lowered the baton into the kerosene. Dip one end. Swipe the rag across the middle. Dip the other end. *Okay. Okay.* Now hold it carefully. Click the lighter. The flame rolls out. One end catches. The other end flames up. *Yes. Yes.*

Now hand it to Devra.

She shoved the flaming baton to Devra. But to her surprise, Devra took a step back. She grabbed her stomach. "Ohhhh." Devra groaned.

What's happening?

Devra's eyes rolled up. She waved the baton away. "I . . . feel sick," Devra said. "Ohh, my stomach. Something wrong." She waved frantically at Gretchen. "Give it to Stacy. I don't feel well."

Holding the baton out in front of her, Gretchen turned to Stacy. The smell of the burning kerosene invaded her nose, strong enough to make her eyes water. Everything suddenly became a blur.

She shoved the baton into Stacy's hand. Stacy flashed her a smile. Stacy spun around and, twirling the baton slowly, ran in front of the stands.

The drummers of the band began a roaring drumroll. Stacy turned to the onlookers in the stands and began to twirl faster. The bright orange-yellow flames danced and darted.

Gretchen began to dip the second baton into the kerosene. She glanced over at Stacy—just as the flames began to roll up Stacy's sleeve. One arm. Then both arms.

The flames shot up her sleeves and over the front of her sweater. They dipped and swirled, sunlight yellow against the purple night sky.

Stacy screamed, a shrill cry of panic, a hoarse, inhuman wail.

She dropped to her knees and the flames shot higher. A jagged, shimmering outline around her writhing body.

Stacy's head was tilted back, her mouth locked open

in wail after wail of horror. Her cries were muffled by the roar and crackle of the flames.

And then Courtney's scream drowned out Stacy's wails. "Somebody help! Stacy's on fire! Help her! Somebody! Stacy's on fire!"

23.

We just want to talk about it," Hernandez said. He motioned for Gretchen to take the leather chair opposite his desk and next to Coach Walker. He carefully closed the door to his inner office.

Gretchen lowered herself into the chair and rubbed her cold, wet hands on the legs of her jeans. Coach Walker kept her eyes on the wall behind the principal's desk. She appeared to be avoiding Gretchen's gaze.

Gretchen cleared her throat. Her mouth suddenly felt so dry. She followed Hernandez as he brushed aside a stack of papers on his desktop, then dropped heavily into his big desk chair.

"Cold in here," Gretchen murmured, rubbing her hands on her legs again.

Coach Walker nodded but didn't reply.

Gretchen noticed a stain on the lapel of the principal's gray suit jacket. Ketchup, maybe? He removed his glasses and wiped the lenses with a red handkerchief. With his glasses off, his eyes looked tiny, she thought, too tiny for his large square face.

The three of them remained silent as Hernandez wiped his glasses. Gretchen heard some girls laughing out in the hall. She wished she could be out there with them.

It was the Monday after the Friday night football game. A weekend of sadness and tension had somehow passed. Gretchen spent most of the time alone in her room with the door closed and music cranked up really loud—to help keep her mother from intruding, and to help drown out her guilt-ridden thoughts.

She wished Sid would come over. Sid could comfort her. Sid could assure her it wasn't entirely her fault, whether that was true or not. Sid could hold her and maybe stop the chills that shook her body, the coldness that gripped her and wouldn't let go.

But he texted that he was at Shadyside General with Stacy and her family. He texted on Saturday that Stacy was in the ICU, that doctors couldn't say how badly she had been hurt. And then on Sunday afternoon, Sid texted that Stacy was "stable," whatever that meant. He said she was being moved to a private room.

Gretchen couldn't breathe any sighs of relief. She had set someone on fire. She didn't really know how it happened. But she had set Stacy on fire, maybe ruined her life forever—if she lived.

If she lived.

That thought made Gretchen's stomach heave, and she had to force her lunch back down.

And then the principal had called her house and asked her to come for a meeting after school on Monday. Thank goodness her mother wasn't home. The call filled Gretchen with troubled questions. Was she going to be suspended from school? Expelled? No. They'd want her mother to be there if that was true.

Would there be police at the meeting? Were Stacy's parents pressing charges?

Attempted murder?

Was Hernandez going to accuse her? Did someone think the whole thing was deliberate?

Gretchen realized she was scaring herself. Hernandez said he was investigating. He didn't say he was accusing her of anything.

And now, here she was facing him, sitting hunched in the chair across from him, her cold hands clasped tightly in her lap, so tightly her fingers ached.

He forced a smile. "Don't look so frightened, Gretchen," he said softly. "We're not here to assign guilt. We just need to know exactly what happened." He scratched one side of his face. "Stacy's parents are going to want to know, too."

"H-how is she?" Gretchen stammered. "Have you heard anything?"

"She's stable, according to the last report I heard," Hernandez said.

"Thank God," Coach Walker murmured.

"She has serious burns over her arms and chest," Hernandez continued, his eyes probing Gretchen's. "The most serious question is if Stacy will regain the use of her right arm again. It's the most badly damaged."

A sob burst from Gretchen's throat. "How awful. I mean—"

"The burn unit at Shadyside General is supposed to be top-notch," Coach Walker said, her gaze on Hernandez. "My cousin was in a car fire, and they performed miracles with him."

"That's good to hear," Hernandez said softly. He picked up a pencil and began rolling it in his fingers. He narrowed his eyes at Gretchen.

Sudden dread tightened her throat. She felt as if she couldn't breathe.

"Any idea how the accident happened?" the principal asked her.

She swallowed. "Uh . . . no. Not really. I mean . . ." Her voice was quivering. Did it make her sound as if she wasn't telling the truth?

"I mean . . . I can't understand it at all. I was so careful. It was my first time doing it, and I wanted to do a perfect job." Gretchen took a breath. Beside her, Coach Walker was now staring at her intently.

"I went over it, step by step," Gretchen continued. "I concentrated on doing it right. I . . . I can't understand. . . ." Her voice cracked.

"Did you see anyone else go near the batons or the kerosene bucket?" Coach Walker asked.

Gretchen thought hard. She shook her head. "No. I don't remember anyone. I . . . I was there the whole time. Well . . ." She suddenly remembered something. "You called me over to the bench, Coach Walker. Remember? You asked if I needed help, and I said no. But that only took a few seconds. I hurried right back."

Coach Walker nodded. She rubbed her chin, swept a hand back through her hair, her face knotted in a frown.

"Gretchen, did you notice anything strange at all? Before or after the accident?"

Gretchen concentrated again. "Well . . . one thing was strange." She hesitated.

Hernandez let go of the pencil. He leaned closer over his desktop. "What was that?"

"Maybe I shouldn't say. . . ." Gretchen murmured.

"Gretchen, anything you think of can be helpful," Coach Walker said. "Don't hold back to protect someone. And don't feel you have to be one-hundred percent positive about something you think you saw. A terrible thing has happened. We need to know why it happened."

Gretchen swallowed again. Her mouth was dry as sandpaper. "Well . . . I'm a little confused about Devra."

"Devra Dalby?" Hernandez sat up straight. He squinted at Gretchen through his glasses. "What about Devra?"

"Devra was supposed to take the first fire baton," Gretchen said. "But when I started to hand it to her, she backed away. She said she didn't feel well. She told me to give it to Stacy."

"I noticed that," Coach Walker said. "I noticed that Devra held back and Stacy ran in front of the stands to perform without her."

"I . . . uh . . . I-I don't want to accuse Devra of anything," Gretchen stammered. "But . . . it was like she *knew* there was something wrong with the baton. I mean, how did she know not to take it?"

A hush fell over the room. Gretchen's words seemed to linger heavily in the air.

Coach Walker rubbed her chin some more, her eyes on the bulletin board behind the principal's desk. Hernandez tapped the pencil against the desktop. He appeared to be faraway, deep in thought.

I had to say it, Gretchen thought. *It was just so strange how Devra wouldn't take the baton. It* couldn't *be a coincidence.*

"We'll talk to Devra later," Hernandez said, finally breaking the silence. He pointed the pencil at Gretchen. "We know that you and Devra have been feuding. We know—"

"Feuding?" Gretchen interrupted.

"Well, you're not exactly best friends," Coach Walker chimed in. "You've accused Devra before. . . ."

Hernandez raised a hand to silence her. "Let me finish. I hate to ask this, Gretchen, but I have to. Coach Walker has told me how eager you were to be on the squad. And we all know that Devra probably doesn't belong there. So tell me this . . ." He hesitated.

Gretchen felt her heart skip a beat. She gripped the leather arms of the chair.

"You didn't try to hand Devra a dangerous baton, hoping to get her off the squad—did you?"

Gretchen gasped. Without thinking, she jumped to her feet. "Of *course* not! That's *horrible!*" she shrieked. "Is that what you think? You think I'm a *killer?*"

A sob escaped Gretchen's throat, and then she couldn't hold back. A flood of tears rolled down her cheeks. She folded herself back into the chair and cried, sobbing hard, her shoulders heaving up and down.

Coach Walker tried to pat her comfortingly on the back. But Gretchen brushed her hand away.

Hernandez sat helplessly, biting his lips, shaking his head. "I'm sorry. It was a question I felt I had to ask."

Gretchen could barely hear him over her sobs. She sucked in breath after breath and finally managed to stop crying. Her cheeks were tear-soaked and burning hot. She wiped her eyes with the palms of her hands.

"I'll never forgive myself," she finally managed to

choke out, not looking at either of them. "I'll never for-give myself for what happened to Stacy. Never."

Gretchen's heavy footsteps echoed down the long, empty hall as she made her way to the exit. She held her breath, struggling not to start crying again. She fumbled in her bag for her car keys, and dropped the bag. She stood watching everything tumble out onto the floor.

"At least the day can't get *worse*," she muttered. She bent down and swept everything back into the bag.

"Hey—!" Gretchen called out, surprised to find Sid waiting for her in the student parking lot. She rushed forward and he wrapped her in his arms.

"I don't need to ask how it went," he said. "I can see your face is a total wreck."

"Thanks a bunch," she muttered. But she pressed her cheek against his chest. She could hear his steady heart-beat. She wondered if hers would ever beat so slow and normal again.

"They think I'm a murderer," she said, raising her eyes to his.

"No way," Sid replied. "You're not serious. They don't think that."

Gretchen sighed. "I don't know what they think. It's all a horrible mystery."

"I just came from the hospital," Sid said.

Gretchen took a step back. "And?"

He shrugged. "Third-degree burns over both arms. It's horrible. She's bandaged up like a mummy."

"Did you talk to her?"

Sid shook his head. "No. She wasn't awake."

Gretchen couldn't help it. The tears began pouring from her eyes again.

Sid stepped forward and wrapped her in a close hug.

And she heard a harsh voice from behind them. "Well! It didn't take *you* long to steal Stacy's boyfriend!"

24.

Gretchen spun away from Sid and stared at Devra's friend Courtney Shaw. Courtney wore a black-and-white-striped T-shirt over white tennis shorts. She had a tennis racket raised in one hand. Her short black hair glistened from sweat. Her silver nose ring flashed in the light of the afternoon sun.

"Courtney, I—" Gretchen couldn't figure out what to say.

"How's it going?" Sid asked casually. As if she hadn't made an accusation. "You have a good game?"

Courtney ignored Sid and glared at Gretchen. "I saw you from the tennis courts." She motioned to the courts at the back of the parking lot. "I just wanted to tell you something."

Gretchen squinted at her. "Tell me something?"

"You're on the cheerleader squad now, right? Because poor Stacy got burned to a crisp?"

Gretchen gasped. "Are you accusing me?"

"Not at all," Courtney said. "I'm just saying."

Gretchen stuck her chin out, ready to defend herself. "Saying what?"

"You're on the squad now, so you and Devra will be together a lot. You probably know that Devra is my good friend."

"So?" Gretchen demanded impatiently.

"So I wanted to warn you. Devra has had enough."

"Are you kidding me?" Gretchen exploded. "Are you out of your mind? Devra has had enough?"

"Listen to me, Gretchen—"

"Devra has been torturing me!" Gretchen shouted. "She has been ruining my life."

"Not true!" Courtney said, slamming her tennis racket against a pole. "Not true! Not true!"

"Can't you both dial it down?" Sid shouted. "I've got sensitive ears."

"Devra doesn't care a thing about you!" Courtney screamed, ignoring Sid. "She isn't interested in you at all. She just wants you to stop blaming her for everything. It's crazy."

"Sending threatening texts isn't crazy?" Gretchen cried. "Cleaning fluid in my water bottle? Jamming my uniform full of cockroaches? And *I'm* the one who's crazy?" She took an angry step toward Courtney. "*You're* the one who's crazy."

Courtney stepped back until she bumped into a car fender. "You've got it all wrong, Gretchen. Devra isn't doing anything to you. I'm telling the truth." She smacked the head of the racket against the ground. "Listen to me. Do you know about the cheerleader retreat?"

"Of course I know about it," Gretchen snapped. "We're all going to stay in these cabins in the woods for a weekend."

"Devra says when we're there, just keep away from her and everything will be okay."

Gretchen pressed her hands against her waist. "She's threatening me?"

"No way. She just wants peace, Gretchen. A truce. Know what I mean? She hasn't done anything to you. She swears it. So just leave her alone." Courtney finished her speech, breathing hard, sweat glistening her short black hair.

Gretchen let out a long breath. "She's a total liar, Courtney. Do you really believe her?"

Courtney didn't answer. She flashed a look of disgust at Sid, swung her racket in the air as if batting him away, turned, and strode off.

Gretchen watched her until she disappeared behind the tennis courts. Suddenly, she felt more confused than ever. Her thoughts whirred through her mind.

If Devra isn't behind all these horrible things . . . then, who? Courtney is lying. She has to be. I know she and Devra are friends. But why would Courtney lie for Devra?

25.

Gretchen and her mother ate dinner in near silence. Mrs. Page was not a good cook, and parts of the roast chicken were nearly raw and the baked potatoes were hard.

Gretchen didn't have much of an appetite, anyway. She hadn't eaten much since the football game. Her stomach was so tightly knotted, she never felt hungry.

The house was so quiet, Gretchen could hear the ticking of the mantelpiece clock in the next room. *I don't know which is worse,* she thought. *Forcing a conversation with my mom, or this horrible silence.*

"I don't know what to say," Mrs. Page said, as if reading Gretchen's thoughts. She set her fork down on the table. "Sorry about the chicken. I knew I should have left it in the oven longer. I get distracted."

"It's . . . okay," Gretchen murmured.

"You can't blame yourself," her mother said, abruptly

changing the subject. "It was a horrible accident, dear. But it *was* an accident."

Gretchen sighed. "That doesn't really help, Mom."

"There's nothing I can say. You tried to be as careful as you could. I know you did."

Gretchen clenched her jaw. "I wasn't careful *enough*." She shoved her plate away. "You're right, Mom. We can't talk about it. It's too awful to talk about."

"You have to put it behind you," Mrs. Page said, licking her lips.

Gretchen hated the way her mother was always licking her lips. Why didn't she wear lip gloss or ChapStick if her lips were so dry? And what was this *put it behind you* nonsense? How stupid was that? What a useless a thing to say.

Gretchen opened her mouth to tell her mother to just stop talking. But her phone rang before she could get a word out. She had the phone on the table in front of her. She picked it up and squinted at the screen. Madison was calling.

Gretchen jumped up. "Mom, I have to take this."

Mrs. Page frowned. "I made dessert. I mean, I bought a pound cake."

"Later." Gretchen gave her a wave and hurried upstairs to her room.

She dropped onto the edge of her bed and pressed the phone to her ear. "Madison—where've you been? I tried calling you all weekend."

"My cousin Emma had a baby," Madison said. "She's the one that lives out on that farm beyond Grove City? My mom wanted to help out, so we spent the weekend there. My phone wouldn't work there. No cells, I guess. And Emma doesn't have WiFi. I've been totally out of touch."

"Oh, wow. I really wanted to talk to you. I—"

"And I need to talk to you," Madison interrupted. "I have to tell you something, Gretchen. Something really horrible."

Gretchen heard her mother coming up the stairs. Was she spying on her?

"Something horrible? Oh my God. Madison, what *is* it?"

"I-I'm supposed to be practicing my violin," Madison stammered. "For the assembly tomorrow morning. But . . . I can't concentrate. I can barely think straight. I . . . I'm so upset."

"Madison—what *is* it?" Gretchen repeated.

"You have to come over. Hurry. I don't want to tell you over the phone."

The bedroom suddenly began to spin. Gretchen shut her eyes to stop her dizziness. *What could be so horrible?*

"Is it about Stacy?" Gretchen demanded, her voice quivering. "Is it?"

"Just hurry over here," Madison insisted.

Gretchen ended the call, tucked the phone into her pocket, and hurried down the stairs, taking them two at a time. Her mother appeared at the front door just as Gretchen was about to pull it open.

How does she do that? Gretchen wondered. *Appear at the door from out of nowhere every time I'm about to leave? She is so annoying!*

"Just going next door." She tried to squeeze past her mother.

"What for?" Mrs. Page demanded, not budging.

"Madison wants to tell me something."

"Sorry." Mrs. Page, hands on hips, shook her head. "You're forgetting your promise."

Gretchen blinked. "Promise?"

"You promised you'd help me with the photo albums tonight. Don't pretend you didn't."

"But, Mom—" Gretchen had her eyes on the door knob. So close yet so far.

"The albums are a mess. In total disarray. You promised you'd help, Gretchen. Tonight's the night. No excuses."

"No, I can't. Really," Gretchen replied, trying to keep her voice low and calm. But she knew she was about to lose it. "Madison—"

"You know I've been obsessing about the albums ever since we moved, Gretchen. It's the next thing on my list, and I want to check it off tonight."

Gretchen let out an exasperated groan. "Mom, you're being really annoying. Madison has something she wants to tell me. We can do the stupid albums tomorrow night!" she screamed.

"Don't you scream at me. Do you think you can convince me by acting like an infant? No way. You're not going out. Whatever your friend has to say can wait, I'm sure. You're staying home and helping me. Keep your promises, Gretchen."

Mrs. Page stood stiffly, whole body tensed, arms crossed tightly in front of her, blocking the door.

"Mom, I swear—"

But Gretchen saw that she had lost.

Do I have the most annoying mother in the world? She's impossible. Impossible!

Her shoulders slumped. She rolled her eyes. "Okay, Mom. Photo albums. If it will make you happy."

Maybe we can get through the albums early, Gretchen thought. *And I can run over to Madison's. Or else I'll have to talk to her after the assembly tomorrow.*

And then questions flashed one after another in her mind.

What is Madison so desperate to tell me?

Is it about Devra?

What could be so horrible?

26.

Gretchen took a seat in the third row of the auditorium next to Ana. She turned to gaze down the rows of seats as kids filed in for the morning assembly. She looked for Sid. He had said something about sitting with her. But he was nowhere to be seen.

Ana held her phone in her lap and was busily texting someone with both thumbs. She held the phone low behind the seatback in front of her because students weren't allowed to use their phones during school hours.

Gretchen glimpsed at Devra at the far end of the row. Devra saw her, too, but quickly glanced away. She and Courtney began talking animatedly, their faces close together.

Ana finished her text and slid the phone into her bag. She shook her head hard, straightening her bangs. "How's it going?"

"A little better," Gretchen said. "I don't know if I'll ever stop thinking about Friday night."

Ana nodded solemnly. "I still hear Stacy's screams in my ears. Last night, I dreamed my house was on fire and I was trapped in my room."

Gretchen shook her head. "Oh, wow. That's terrible."

The auditorium lights dimmed. Principal Hernandez, in his gray suit, strode up the stairs at the side of the stage.

"Did Coach Walker tell you?" Ana asked. "Hernandez banned fire batons. We can't perform with them anymore."

"I guess he's right," Gretchen murmured.

It's all my fault, she thought.

She realized Ana was staring at her intently, studying her. She wondered what Ana was really thinking. Did she think Gretchen was a careless idiot who should be punished for what happened to Stacy? Is that what everyone in school thought?

Or was Gretchen being paranoid?

Stacy was so pretty and lively and funny and energetic. Everyone likes Stacy. And now I'm going to be remembered for the rest of my time here as the idiot girl who set Stacy on fire.

"Have you been to the hospital?" Ana asked. "Did you go see Stacy?"

"Well . . . no," Gretchen answered, avoiding Ana's gaze. "But Sid gives me reports about her."

Ana's eyes widened in surprise. "You talk to Sid? You've been hanging out with him?"

"Kind of."

Gretchen swallowed. Did she just say something

wrong? Ana seemed more than surprised. Her questions sounded like an accusation.

Ana appeared to be studying her even more intently. Gretchen was glad that the auditorium had gone dark, and Hernandez was stepping up behind a podium at the side of the stage.

Four musicians, two men and two women, wearing black suits and white shirts, had taken their seats, facing each other on folding chairs in the center of the stage. The woman holding a tall cello was busily tuning it. The two men sat casually, chatting, violins perched in their laps.

It took Hernandez a while to get everyone quiet. Some guys in the back row were loudly doing a rap song that Gretchen had heard on the radio, pounding the seats in rhythm with their beats, and others were laughing and cheering them on.

"We're going to enjoy a *different* kind of music this morning," Hernandez told them, bringing his mouth too close to the microphone so that his words made popping sounds as he spoke.

"But that's a classic!" a guy in the back row shouted. Laughter spread down the rows of seats.

Hernandez raised both hands above his head and kept them there until everyone was silent. "We have a special treat this morning," he announced. "The four members of the Chicagoland Arts String Quartet have graciously come to our school to perform for us."

A mild burst of applause greeted his announcement. Onstage, the four musicians sat upright, readying their instruments.

"And to make this concert really special," Hernandez continued, "one of the eleventh-graders from our orchestra will be joining the quartet."

Gretchen suddenly felt tense. This was Madison's big moment. She must be so nervous now, Gretchen knew. *Maybe that's why Madison wanted me to come over last night. Just to help her get over her nerves.*

Gretchen was suddenly feeling it, too. "Go, Madison! Go, Madison!" she chanted to herself.

"Let's bring Madison Grossman out to join the quartet," Hernandez said. He motioned with both hands, and everyone applauded.

Madison strode onto the stage. She wore a white blouse, pleated in the front like a tuxedo shirt, and a long black skirt. She had put her hair up high on her head. She took a funny, exaggerated bow, reacting to the applause, and everyone laughed. The laughter seemed to relax her, and she smiled for the first time.

"Madison is going to join the quartet to play . . ." Hernandez raised a sheet of paper to his face and read, ". . . the first two movements of the Mozart Viennese String Quartet Number Eight."

A pleased smile crossed his face. He gestured to the musicians, turned, and walked off the stage.

Madison sat down on the empty chair facing the cello

player. Her violin case stood beside the chair. She bent and raised the case to her lap. One of the women said something to her, and Madison laughed.

She opened the case and lifted out the violin and the bow. Then she snapped the case shut and returned it to the floor beside her chair.

The cello player said something to her. From her seat in the third row in the audience, Gretchen couldn't hear what they were saying. Some kids shifted in their seats impatiently.

The musicians raised their instruments. The male violinist tapped his bow twice on his instrument. They began to play.

Gretchen watched Madison. Madison's face was tight, intense, her eyes narrowed on the music stand in front of her. Sitting up straight and stiff, she counted off several measures. Then she raised the violin to her chin.

Gretchen relaxed a little. *Madison is doing it. She's going to be great.*

The melodic flow of the strings floated over the auditorium. Gretchen slid down in her seat and raised her knees to the seatback in front of her.

The music was sweet, gentle, very rhythmic and precise.

It lasted only thirty seconds. Then a hideous, high animal scream, a shrill bleat of shock and pain, shot over the auditorium and rang off the walls.

It took Gretchen a few seconds to realize that Madison was the one shrieking and crying.

Madison leaped to her feet and tossed her violin across the stage. She grabbed her neck and dropped to her knees. Cry after cry burst from her throat.

The four musicians jumped up, too. They stumbled back, eyes wide with shock, staring down at Madison as she held her neck and screamed.

"I'm burning! It's *burning*! Somebody! Help me! Help! I'm burning!"

Screams rang out across the auditorium. Teachers ran toward the stage.

Gretchen jumped to her feet. She could see that Madison's neck was a flaming red. Madison gave out one last shriek and, gripping her neck, fell sideways, collapsed to the floor. Bright red blood gushed up from her neck like a fountain. The blood shot up in a wave of scarlet and then splashed down on the stage floor, splashed all around her. Madison didn't move.

Principal Hernandez was running across the stage now, his necktie flying over his shoulder. He pushed one of the shocked musicians aside and dropped to the stage floor beside Madison.

A horrified hush fell over the auditorium. It was as if someone had taken the volume knob and turned it all the way down to silent. Students stood, gaping wide-eyed, pressing their hands over the seatbacks in front of them.

It was so quiet, Gretchen could hear Hernandez's

imploring pleas as he leaned over Madison, his face close to hers. "Madison? Madison? Please answer me. Can you hear me? Madison?"

Gretchen realized she'd been holding her breath. Her hands were clenched into tight fists. Her stomach had knotted in dread.

"Call a doctor!" a teacher shouted from the edge of the stage.

"Somebody—call 911!" someone else cried.

Leaning over Madison, Hernandez raised a hand. "It may be too late," he said. "She's not breathing."

27.

Sid wrapped his arm around Gretchen. She slid against him and pressed her head against his shoulder.

I want to disappear, she thought. *I want Sid to wrap his arms around me, shut out the light, and I'll disappear forever.*

The real world was too hard to face, Gretchen decided. Too horrifying and cruel.

"How could someone murder Madison?" Her words came out in a choked whisper. She hadn't been able to think of anything else since yesterday morning in the auditorium. Just kept asking herself the same question again and again.

And what a cold-blooded, horrifying murder it was. Someone had doused acid over the chin rest of Madison's violin. Enough acid to burn right through Madison's neck. It had burned through Madison's aorta, and Madison had bled to death before anything could be done.

About as cold and cruel as a murder can get. And Gretchen knew she had no proof. But the only person she knew who had acid was Devra Dalby. Acid powerful enough to burn paint off furniture.

She snuggled against Sid's chest. His warmth wasn't enough to stop her chills.

"The school building is completely closed off," Sid said, shaking his head. "The Shadyside police are everywhere, and they are talking to everyone."

"They haven't talked to *me* yet," Gretchen said, her voice muffled against his chest. "I . . . I need to talk with them."

Sid's body went tense. "Why? What do you know?"

Gretchen pulled away from him. She sat up, arranging her hair behind her shoulders. She knew she looked a mess. She hadn't even brushed her hair this morning. And her eyes were red and puffy from crying, her cheeks tear-stained and pale.

She wore the jeans, torn at the knees, she'd been wearing all week. And a sweatshirt with orange food stains on the front that she'd pulled out of her laundry bag. She didn't care how she looked. Her friend was dead. DEAD. Murdered.

She couldn't stop picturing the gusher of bright blood shooting up from Madison's open throat, spouting over Madison and splashing onto the stage floor. She couldn't stop hearing again and again the screams and horrified shrieks of everyone in the auditorium as they looked helplessly on.

Sid waited patiently for her to explain.

Gretchen took a deep, shuddering breath. "Madison called me the night before the music assembly," she began. "She sounded kind of frantic. She said she had something important to tell me, something she didn't want to tell me over the phone."

Sid frowned at her. "What was it?"

"I-I don't know," Gretchen stammered. "I started over to her house, and my mother stopped me. She wouldn't let me go over there." She uttered a low growl. "So typical. She's just always in my way."

Sid patted her hand. "Let's leave your mother out of this," he said softly. "You have no clue as to what Madison wanted to tell you?"

"No clue." Gretchen lowered her eyes to the floor and stifled a sob. She'd already cried so much. She was desperate not to start again.

Sid swept a hand back through his dark hair. "Do you think Madison was killed because of what she wanted to tell you? Do you think someone killed her to shut her up?"

"Wait. I have to tell you this. A while ago, Devra told me she had a powerful acid," Gretchen blurted out. She had been holding that information in for too long. Just knowing it felt as if it was burning a hole in her.

Sid's mouth dropped open. "Excuse me? Say that again."

"I was at Lefty's. Devra sat down at my table. She wanted to bribe me not to win the cheerleader tryout.

And she said she was working on a cabinet to surprise her dad. She told me she was using acid to remove the paint."

Sid stared blankly at her, as if her words didn't make sense to him.

"Don't you see?" Gretchen urged impatiently. "Don't you see?" She tugged his sleeve. "A while ago, Madison told me she knew some things about Devra."

"Some *things*? Like what?"

"She never told me," Gretchen said. "Maybe she wanted to tell me the night before she was killed. And—"

"And Devra doused Madison's violin with acid to keep her from telling?"

"It sounds crazy. . . ." Gretchen said softly.

"Yeah. Crazy," Sid murmured. "Devra is a crazed killer? Crazy."

"Hernandez and Coach Walker questioned me about Stacy," Gretchen said, squeezing her fingers around his arm, as if holding on to a life raft. "I told them my suspicions about Devra. I mean, why Devra backed away and didn't take the fire baton, so Stacy had to take it."

"And what did they say?"

"They said they'd talk to Devra. But nothing came of it. They probably thought I was just trying to get Devra in trouble. You know. Because of the competition, because of the troubles between us."

Sid shook his head. "It's hard to believe. Devra burned Stacy and murdered Madison? That's like . . . impossible." He turned to her. "But you do have to tell the police what you suspect. I mean, lots of people could buy acid. Just because Devra was using acid doesn't mean . . ." His voice trailed off. "But what if you're right? What if Devra really is crazy? What if she really did those things?"

Gretchen could see his mind spinning. She could tell he didn't want to believe that Devra was a cold-blooded murderer. The whole idea that someone they knew could deliberately kill . . .

"Shouldn't you be at the hospital? What about Stacy?" Gretchen asked suddenly.

Sid didn't answer. Instead, he wrapped her in a tight hug. They kissed.

"Stacy and I . . . I told you, it's over," he said when the kiss ended. "It's over but she refuses to accept it. I told you. And as long as she's in the hospital, I can't really fight with her or argue or try to make her see the truth."

He sighed. "I have to be there with her. I can't upset her. She's . . . she's really messed up."

They held onto each other. They kissed again.

Sid stood up to leave. "I'm sorry. I have to go check in on Stacy."

Gretchen's mind was still on what they had talked about. "What if Devra really is a murderer? And we're the only ones who know it? What does that mean? What does it mean, Sid?"

He stared at her. "That she'll come after *us* next."

28.

"Polly—I wish you were here." Gretchen gazed into her laptop screen.

"But FaceTime is almost as good," Polly said.

"Did you add highlights to your hair?"

Polly grinned. "Think it works?"

"Definitely."

Gretchen studied her friend on the screen. Polly was so light and small. With her flood of auburn curls bouncing on her round face, pale creamy cheeks, and those huge brown eyes, she looked like a little doll. Everything about her said energy and dynamo and electricity and pep.

She was the best cheerleader at Savanna Mills. So light and springy and a total daredevil. Gretchen sometimes felt like an elephant beside her, although Polly never stopped talking about how much she admired Gretchen's skill and athleticism and mature good looks.

A perfect team.

"So tell me what's happening," Polly said, her expression turning serious. "This must have been a total nightmare for you, Gretchen."

Gretchen nodded and once again stifled a sob. "Madison was my friend, the only friend I've made in Shadyside."

Polly brushed a strand of curls off her forehead. "Have they caught the murderer?"

Gretchen shook her head. "It's Devra Dalby. I told you on the phone last night, I know it's Devra. I'm so terrified. I'm the only one who knows."

Gretchen raised her eyes to the clock over the sink. "I have to go to a cheerleader meeting in a little while. I . . . I'm dreading it, Polly. I'm afraid to be in the same room with Devra."

"And what about the retreat?" Polly asked." You said there was a cheerleader retreat . . . ?"

Gretchen nodded. "Can you imagine? We're all going to be staying in cabins in the woods. In the woods with a crazed killer? A crazed killer who *hates* me. I'm so scared, Polly, I can't even think about it."

"Did you talk to the cheerleader coach?" Polly asked. "Did you talk to the police?"

"I finally talked to two officers last night," Gretchen said. "I told them everything. About the acid Devra was using on a cabinet. Everything."

"And?"

"They said they were following all leads." Gretchen

sighed. "They were very nice. I told them what good friends Madison and I were. I think they were being careful not to upset me. But they didn't seem terribly interested in what I had to say."

"Weird," Polly muttered. "And are they opening your school again?"

Gretchen nodded. "Tomorrow. It's been closed for two days. But it's opening tomorrow, and guess what? The principal decided to go ahead with the football game Friday night."

Polly's eyes widened in surprise. "Really?"

"Really. He said it would be good for school morale."

Polly twisted a corner of her mouth up as she thought about that. A tiny dimple formed in her cheek. *She really does look like a toy doll,* Gretchen thought, even when she's being totally serious and thoughtful.

She's so sweet. The best friend I could ever have.

"I have to go to the cheerleader meeting," Gretchen said. "I'm so glad we had a chance to talk. It really helps, Polly. It really does."

Gretchen clicked off the connection. She had to drive to school now. She had to see what Coach Walker had to say to the cheerleaders. She had to stand in the same space as Devra Dalby.

Was she in total danger? She never dreamed she'd be in the same room as a murderer.

And one chilling question kept repeating in her mind: Would Devra kill again?

29.

Gretchen drove through a gray afternoon, rain clouds low in the sky. A few raindrops drizzled onto the windshield. Gusts of wind sent dead brown leaves toppling from the trees, dancing in the air as they fell.

The high school was dark, she noticed, as she slowed and pulled the car around the side of the building to the student parking lot. Only two other cars parked back here. And a single black-and-white police cruiser parked at an angle at the back entrance.

Why are the police still here? It's three days later. What could they possibly find?

She tried to shake her thoughts from her mind as she entered the empty building. The hallway was dimly lit and cold, as if they had turned off the heat while everyone was away.

The gym was even colder. Coach Walker was scurrying along the wall, turning on lights. Basketballs, normally stacked in the equipment room, were scattered across the gym floor as if they'd escaped their prison.

Gretchen spotted Courtney doing stretching exercises on the floor in front of the coach's office. Ana and Devra were against the far wall, chatting quietly. Becka and Shannon sat cross-legged on the floor, backs against the wall, studying their phones.

Gretchen looked for Sid, but then remembered he hadn't been invited to this meeting. She swung her bag off her shoulder and tossed it against the wall. She rubbed her hands together, trying to warm them. "You can almost see your breath in here," she told Coach Walker.

Walker nodded. "I think the school was trying to save money while no one was here. I don't think they ran the furnace at all." She stopped and studied Gretchen. "How are you doing? I mean, seriously."

"Seriously, not so great," Gretchen said. "It's kind of weird being back in this building."

"Did you see one of the counselors the school made available?" the coach asked.

Gretchen stared at her. *What could a counselor tell me? Not to be upset even though a good friend was murdered in front of my eyes?*

"No," Gretchen answered simply.

She glanced to the far wall and saw that Devra had turned away from Ana. Devra was watching Gretchen now. Staring hard. Her face a blank.

Why is she looking at me?

"I think getting back to a normal schedule is the best thing we can do," Walker said. She rearranged the baseball cap on her head. "I mean, no way we can forget what happened. But we have to get past it."

She didn't wait for Gretchen to reply. She motioned with both hands for the other cheerleaders to gather around.

"We're not going to practice today," the coach announced. "I think we're prepared for the game against the Bisons tomorrow night. I know nothing feels normal, and we all have a million questions, and we're all troubled and tense because of the horrible thing that happened in our school. But I think we have an important job to do, all of us. And I asked Courtney to say a few words."

Courtney swept a hand back over her short hair. She stepped into the center of the circle of girls, adjusting the sleeves of her Shadyside High jersey.

"I agree with Coach Walker," she started. "We cheerleaders have an important job to do. We can help get our school back on track. I mean, this week has been the pits, and I think everyone in school feels terrible. There've been a lot of tears and a lot of nightmares and a lot of sadness."

Her voice cracked. She took a breath. "First Stacy has a horrible accident. Then Madison is murdered onstage. How can we ever recover from that? How can our school return to just a little bit of normal?"

Her eyes swept the circle of girls. "I think that's where *we* come in. I mean, we're cheerleaders. That means we're the spirit leaders of the school. I thought about this a lot when Coach Walker asked me to speak. Everyone talks about school spirit. But what is it really?

"It isn't just a slogan. It means the feeling of the school. How the students here feel about themselves and about our high school. And I think if we do a good job at the game Friday night . . . if we get everyone really yelling and screaming and cheering . . . we will do our part in lifting everyone's spirits."

Courtney glanced around the circle again, as if checking if everyone was with her. "That's what cheerleaders can do," she continued. "A lot of people think cheerleading is old-fashioned or sexist or dumb. But I think we can show that they are wrong. We have a real purpose. Maybe we can call it a goal. And that's to get everyone here out of the dumps and get them cheering again."

Courtney let out a relieved sigh. She stepped back. She had an uncertain expression on her face. *Maybe she was expecting us all to burst into applause,* Gretchen thought.

The girls remained silent. Finally, Ana spoke up. "I agree with Courtney. Good job, Courtney. You made me feel better already." The others murmured agreement. A smile slowly spread over Courtney's face.

"Yes, good job, Courtney," Coach Walker chimed in. "I think you described our mission perfectly. I'd say you were even eloquent."

Courtney's cheeks turned pink. "Thank you. I gave it a lot of thought."

"And you had another thought," Walker said. "About Gretchen."

Gretchen stiffened at the sound of her name. Why was Courtney thinking about Gretchen? She knew Courtney wasn't her friend. Courtney was Devra's friend. She and Gretchen had never said a kind word to one another.

Courtney cleared her throat, her eyes on Gretchen. "Well, I just thought we should do something different for the crowd Friday night, something special. I mean, if we do something totally awesome, we can really get them shouting."

"Tell them your idea," Coach Walker said.

"Coach Walker and I were watching your highlight video," Courtney said, turning to Gretchen. "From your old school. And we both totally couldn't believe your Double Flying Somersault. Has anyone else here seen it?"

To Gretchen's surprise, Devra raised her hand.

Why was Devra watching my highlight reel?

"Well . . ." Courtney continued, "You flew up so high, it was totally amazing, Gretchen."

"You have to jump pretty high to do a double," Gretchen said.

"Well, Coach and I thought you could do it Friday at the game and . . . just blow everyone away. I mean, it could be so awesome."

Gretchen glimpsed a look of disgust on Devra's face.

"What do you think?" Coach Walker asked Gretchen.

Gretchen felt her face turning red. She hated the fact that she blushed so easily. But having all eyes suddenly on her got her heart pumping. "I have a better idea," she said. "Why don't I teach it to someone else, and we can *both* do it Friday night? That would be even more spectacular, right?"

Walker shook her head. "Nice thought, but I don't think we have time. The only time we have to practice it is after eighth period tomorrow."

Gretchen hesitated. "Well . . ."

"You'll have time to teach it to the others before the state tournament," Walker suggested. "We could really wow the judges."

"I guess I can do it Friday night," Gretchen said, still thinking hard about it. "But I need a really strong catcher. I come down really fast, and the timing has to be perfect."

Courtney shook her head. "Too bad. That's a problem. Stacy was our best catcher."

Silence.

Then: "Devra, do you think *you* could catch Gretchen?" Coach Walker asked.

Gretchen gasped. *Coach Walker—what are you trying to do? KILL me?*

30.

Where are we going?" Gretchen fiddled with the cigarette lighter on the dashboard. Sid's Pontiac was so old, it had a cigarette lighter. And a cassette player.

"Just driving around," Sid answered, slowing for a stop sign. He had one hand on the wheel, one hand on her thigh.

"Let go of me," Gretchen said, gently removing his hand. "Watch where you're going."

Sid turned onto Park Drive. He had waited for her after the cheerleader meeting and suggested they take a drive.

The late afternoon sun was slipping behind the trees, sending rays of shimmering red through the nearly bare branches. "Finish your story," he demanded. "Walker asked Devra to catch you. And what did Devra say?"

Gretchen snickered. "She said no. You could have knocked me over. She had this perfect opportunity to drop me on my head, and she turned it down."

"Weird," Sid murmured.

"She said she hurt her shoulder at her tennis lesson, and she didn't think she could do it," Gretchen told him. She slumped in the seat, the scratchy seat cover rubbing her back, and lifted her knees to the dashboard.

"Weird," Sid repeated. He made a whistling sound through his lips. "Maybe she has something worse planned for you."

"Worse than dropping me on my head?"

"Maybe she's waiting for the cheerleader retreat."

"Maybe," Gretchen said in a whisper.

He followed the sloping curve of the road, picking up speed, passing a slow-moving SUV filled with little kids.

"So you're not going to do your famous Double Somersault?"

"No, I'm doing it. Shannon said she'd catch me. She's been working out, working on her upper body strength for gymnastics."

"Shannon is awesome," Sid murmured, eyes crinkling as a smile crossed his face.

"Shut up," Gretchen said, giving him a slap on the arm. "She seems nice. I don't really know her. She and Becka sort of hang by themselves."

Gretchen gasped as Sid swerved hard. She saw the dog running in the road, a large German shepherd. Sid had swerved to miss it.

"That dog is lost," she said. "Look. It doesn't have a collar."

GIVE ME A K-I-L-L

"Almost hit it," Sid said. "It's as big as a deer."

"Where are we going?" Gretchen asked, still breathless.

"I thought we'd park up at River Ridge." He grinned at her, moving his eyebrows up and down.

"I don't think so," she said. "Mom is expecting me for dinner. And I have homework since school is starting up again. Did you forget homework?"

"What's for dinner?" Sid asked. "Maybe I'll join you."

"You're not invited." She hit him again. "Hey, how come we never go to your house?"

His grin faded instantly. "We can't," he said softly, eyes narrowing on the curving road ahead of them. "My dad is always there, and he's a beast most of the time."

Gretchen laughed. "He's a beast?"

"Not funny." Sid's hard expression didn't change. "Ever since he lost his job, he takes it out on me and Mom."

"When did he lose his job?" Gretchen asked. "What does he do?"

"Don't go there," Sid said, his jaw tight. "I don't want to talk about it."

"No. Really."

"I don't want to talk about it." He slammed his shoe on the gas pedal, and the old Pontiac roared and lurched, and then shot forward, up the River Road.

Confused, Gretchen turned away from him. She gazed out the window, at the darkening waters of the

Conononka River below as the sun disappeared behind the tall pine trees.

Okay. He doesn't want to talk about it. Fine.

But he doesn't have to bite my head off.

Their first angry words. And she had no idea why he was angry.

"My mom is kind of a beast, too," she said, still turned to the window. "I mean, I'd invite you to dinner, but you wouldn't like her at all."

Sid didn't reply.

"She's totally negative." Gretchen continued anyway. "A total downer. All the time. She never says anything cheerful or encouraging. Always just puts me down and tries to make me feel small."

"Bad news," Sid murmured.

"I really have to get home," Gretchen said, turning back to him. "I'm sorry if I said something to get you angry, but—"

"No worries," he said. He forced a smile. "It's just my dad is kind of a bad subject right now. I'm . . . uh . . . well, I'm trying to work things out, you know?"

"Okay."

The River Road widened to two lanes. Sid waited for a truck to rumble past. Then he made a wide U-turn and started back the way they had come.

Gretchen squeezed his hand, eager to pull him out of his sudden black mood. "One good thing about the halftime show," she said. "No fire batons. You won't have to worry about a kerosene bucket and all that."

He nodded. "Yeah. Guess my job is easier now." He turned his eyes to her. "That reminds me. I was at the hospital. Some good news. Stacy has the use of her right hand back."

Gretchen swallowed. "You mean—"

"They thought maybe she'd never be able to use it," Sid said, turning back to the winding road in front of them. "But she can move her fingers now. It should be okay."

"I didn't know—"

"You should go visit her," Sid said. "You're the only girl on the squad who hasn't been to the hospital."

"I'm the only girl who set her on fire," Gretchen said, her stomach suddenly heavy with dread. "No way she wants to see me. I'm sure she blames me. I couldn't go there, Sid. I couldn't—"

"She knows it was an accident," he said.

Gretchen shook her head. "No. I can't do it. I can't visit her. First I set her on fire. Then I stole her boyfriend." She leaned forward in the seat. "Have you told Stacy about us?"

"Not yet," Sid answered quickly. "It isn't the right time. She's concentrating so hard on getting better. I don't want to do anything to spoil it."

I'll bet Courtney told her, Gretchen thought.

Sid turned the car onto Fear Street. The old trees arching over the road made it suddenly seem dark as night. High on their wide lawns, the big houses rolled past. The shrill screech of a cat somewhere nearby sounded over the rumble of the car engine.

Sid pulled to the curb in front of Gretchen's house. He turned in his seat and squeezed her hand. "I was serious about Devra planning something for you at the cheerleader retreat," he said, dark eyes exploring her face. "Maybe you shouldn't go to the retreat."

Gretchen shook her head. "I *have* to go," she said. "I really don't have a choice."

"But if she's killed once . . ." Sid started.

Gretchen raised a hand to silence him. "First I have to survive my Double Somersault," she said.

31.

Gretchen tugged down the sleeves of her maroon-and-white uniform sweater as she trotted after the other girls into the stadium. The lights cut through the thin layer of fog that had washed in earlier that evening. *The stadium appears as bright as a dream,* she thought.

The two teams were warming up at opposite ends of the field. A Tigers player let a long pass sail over his head, and the ball bounced in front of Gretchen. Without breaking stride, she kicked it back onto the field.

That brought her a few cheers from the stands. She turned and saw that the home seats were only about two-thirds filled, a smaller crowd than usual.

"Some of the parents were protesting," a voice said in her ear. Gretchen turned to see Coach Walker trotting beside her. Their shoes crunched on the gravel of the running track that circled the field. "A few parents believed it was too soon after Madison's death. They wanted us to cancel the game."

Gretchen's eyes swept the empty seats. "I guess some people stayed away."

"Maybe the weather kept them away," Walker said. "This fog. And it's cold for October."

The cheerleaders formed a line in front of the stands and began to perform a warm-up cheer.

"Give me a T
Give me an I
Give m a G
Give me an E
Give me an R!
What does that spell?
What does that spell?
It spells ROOOOOAAAAAAR!
Go, Tigers!"

Mild applause. A few shouts. People were still arriving. In the bleachers to the right, the Shadyside High band started to play a march that Gretchen didn't recognize. The sound was muffled by the fog. The stadium lights appeared to flicker, but Gretchen saw that was caused by shadows from the fog.

Everything seems unreal tonight. Everything is just a little bit weird.

A hand grabbed her shoulder. Coach Walker pulled her aside. "Tell me about your practice this afternoon." She shouted over the tinny blare of the band. "Do you think you're ready to do the Double Somersault?"

"Ready as I'll ever be," Gretchen joked.

"Seriously," Walker said. "Do you think Becka and Shannon can handle it? Be honest, Gretchen. Are you confident? If you're not up to it, we can postpone it. Do it later in the year."

Gretchen nodded. "We practiced for an hour. They're both pretty strong. They give me a good hard boost to send me up, and Shannon didn't have any trouble catching me as I landed."

The band ended the march and began a brassy version of "Beat It," the Michael Jackson song. Gretchen watched Sid handing out maroon-and-white pom-poms to the other girls.

"You landed on your feet every time?" Coach Walker demanded.

Gretchen nodded again. "Shannon had to straighten me out a few times. She was very good."

"Okay." Walker patted Gretchen's shoulder. "Do it. It will be a big boost for everyone, I think. But, listen . . ." She brought her face close to Gretchen's. "If you feel anything is wrong at all, don't try for the double. Just do a single. That will be spectacular enough. Okay?"

"Okay," Gretchen agreed. She could see the concern

on Walker's face. Two tragedies in the school this fall were more than enough. The coach obviously didn't want Gretchen to become another.

The cheerleaders were doing another welcome cheer. Gretchen ran to Sid to get her pom-poms. He flashed her a thumbs-up. "Everything good?"

"So far," she said. "Practice was good. I feel good."

He looked around. "Do you believe this fog? Where did it come from?"

Gretchen turned and saw Devra watching her, pom-poms pressed to her waist, eyes narrowed, her expression hard. Devra's red hair had come loose and was blowing wildly around her head. She pushed it down and, with a final glance at Gretchen, turned back to the stands.

Gretchen hurried to join the line of cheerleaders. The game was about to begin, but the stands were still about a third empty. The lights overhead suddenly appeared brighter. Everything snapped into focus. She realized the fog had lifted.

Right in time for the game.

Whistles blew. The two teams broke their huddles on the field and began to line up.

"We're the Tigers and we like to roar!
We're the Tigers and we like to score!
What do we want? More!
What do we do? SCORE!
Go, Tigers!"

The first half flew by. Gretchen concentrated on the cheers and sideline routines. She concentrated on being a teammate. She forced thoughts of her Double Somersault from her mind.

Leaping high with the other girls, shouting, urging the crowd to cheer—it gave her a strong feeling of confidence she didn't normally feel. That was one reason she loved cheerleading. She became someone else. Her doubts and negative feelings and worries disappeared.

She was an athlete. A performer. A member of a team.

Her good feeling lasted until halftime.

32.

A light drizzle had started to fall. Ponchos and rain gear appeared in the stands. A few people headed for the parking lot, but the score was tied 14–14, so most people stayed.

The Tigers marching band took the field with their *Star Wars* halftime show. Gretchen had heard them practicing and wished she could watch the show. She loved the music from *Star Wars*. Two white-helmeted stormtroopers led the band into its formations.

Gretchen turned away to huddle with the other cheerleaders. Their tradition was to form a circle and hold hands before their halftime routine. Beside Gretchen, Ana was trembling. "So cold," she murmured, brushing raindrops off her forehead.

"We'll warm up once we start our routines," Gretchen told her.

"Showtime, everyone," Coach Walker called, as the

band marched off the field, following the stormtroopers back to the bleachers.

The cheerleaders ran in front of the stands, cheering and shouting. Gretchen took her place in the center of the line. She could feel excitement making her blood pulse. A surge of energy shot through her body.

This is what I love.

She was halfway through the first cheer when she spotted Shannon at the far end of the line. *Whoa. Wait a minute.*

Becka stood at Gretchen's left, doing her arm motions as she shouted the cheer. Shannon was supposed to be at Gretchen's right. Had she forgotten her role in Gretchen's Double Somersault?

They began the new rap cheer that they had practiced earlier in the week. The crowd quieted for this one. Maybe because it was new.

Gretchen nearly lost her place when she saw who stood at her right. Devra? Why was Devra in Shannon's spot?

The rap cheer ended and applause echoed down the rows of benches. Despite the cold drizzle, the crowd was warming up.

Gretchen turned to Devra. "I have to do my somersault now," she said. She meant for Devra to move away so Shannon could take the spot.

But Devra nodded. "Okay."

Gretchen started to protest. "Shannon—"

"Hurt her ankle," Devra interrupted. "I said I could catch you. No problem."

No problem?

Gretchen shuddered. She saw Shannon jumping up and down at the end of the line. Her ankle didn't appear to be hurt.

"Ready, Gretchen?" Coach Walker shouted from the sidelines.

"Ready, Gretchen?" Devra repeated, a cold smile on her face.

Gretchen felt a wave of panic rise up her body. Her muscles tightened. She knew what Devra planned. Devra planned to drop her on her head.

What had Devra said to Shannon? Had she threatened her? Bribed her? A gift certificate at Dalby's Department Store? How had she persuaded Shannon to step aside so that Devra could injure Gretchen?

She'll make it look like a terrible accident. No one will believe she dropped me deliberately.

I can't do this. I have to say no.

But she saw Coach Walker staring at her. The crowd had lost interest. People had turned away from the field, talking and laughing, slapping their hands together to keep warm.

Gretchen flashed a questioning look at Becka. Becka shrugged in reply.

I guess I have to do this. I promised Coach Walker.

But will Devra catch me?

Gretchen shut her eyes and took a deep breath. She nodded to the other cheerleaders. She decided she had no choice. They began the cheer.

Tigers ROAR
Bisons WEEP!
Tigers SOAR
*TIGERS **LEAP**!*

At the shouted word *leap,* Becka and Devra gave Gretchen a high boost. Arms straight up, she jumped off their hands and went flying into the air. No thinking now. No time to think. Her muscles did the thinking. Her muscles knew the routine.

And now she appeared to float for a few seconds. High above them. And then she was leaning forward. Head down. One somersault. Two. Two breathless somersaults. With no thinking. No time. No time. Flashes of color. A pounding heartbeat. No time to breathe or think.

Defying gravity, her body flipped once. Twice.

And then she came down, screaming all the way.

33.

Devra caught Gretchen, wrapping her arms around her waist. Gretchen landed hard, her knees bending as her shoes hit the ground. It took a few seconds to gain her balance. Then she ran to the sidelines, following the other girls. Her heart was pumping in her ears, too loud to hear the shouts and applause of the crowd.

Coach Walker slapped Gretchen on the back as she ran past. "Perfect!" she cried. "A perfect ten!"

A wave of nausea rolled over Gretchen. She held her breath, forcing it down. The stadium lights flashed in her eyes. Her blood pulsed in her ears, refused to fade.

I did it.

"Why did you scream like that?" Devra demanded, one hand on Gretchen's shoulder. "What was *that* about?"

You know what it was about. You attacked me in the gym that night in the dark—and you deliberately tried to terrify me tonight.

That's what Gretchen wanted to say.

Instead, she shrugged. "Just wanted to make it more exciting," she said.

Devra's eyes burned into hers. Devra had a strange smile on her face. A smile of triumph, Gretchen guessed.

She scared me without hurting me. That smile says this won't be the end of it. She has something planned for me. She's waiting for the retreat.

"So you can't come over?" Gretchen pressed the phone to her ear. "I know it's late, Sid. But I can't get to sleep. The adrenaline rush from the game. You know."

She glimpsed the old-fashioned-looking wooden clock on the bookshelf. Twelve-fifteen. She curled her bare feet under her, sitting sideways on the big leather armchair in the den.

Sid's voice sounded tired, hoarse. "Is your mom home?"

Gretchen snickered. "Why do you care?" She didn't give him time to answer. "Actually, Mom is out on a date. Some guy she met at the Pick-N-Pay. Seriously. I think she picked him up."

"Is your mom hot?" Sid asked.

Gretchen's mouth dropped open. "Never thought about it. I guess she's okay. She's got a good body, for forty-five. I mean, she's thin, you know. And she's got great hair. But her expression is always so droopy. Her face is like, Keep Away from Me or You'll Be Sorry."

"Maybe you know her too well," Sid said.

That didn't make a lot of sense to Gretchen. "Yeah. Maybe. Maybe they're hooking up and she won't even be home tonight. Ha. That's a laugh."

"My dad is yelling at me to get off the phone," Sid said. "Can you hear him? He keeps shouting at me, 'Don't you know what time it is?'"

"Well, okay. Bye." Gretchen started to end the call. Then she remembered. "But you're coming over to help me tomorrow, right?"

A brief silence. Then: "Oh. Right. Clean your garage. Did I really say yes to that? Yeah. Okay."

"Well, don't sound so enthusiastic," Gretchen said. "You *said* you'd come over and help."

"Did I promise, or did I just say?" Sid replied.

"Shut up."

He laughed. "I'll be there. Do I get to meet your mom? I hear she's hot."

"Shut up again, Sid. You're getting annoying."

Sid showed up at Gretchen's house a little after one thirty on Saturday afternoon, dressed in faded jeans torn at both knees and an oversized gray sweatshirt, ready for garage cleanup duty.

Mrs. Page behaved very well. She didn't embarrass Gretchen as she usually did in front of her friends. Gretchen chalked it up to her mom's being tired after her date.

Mrs. Page did make a comment about how dumb you have to be to buy jeans that are already ripped. And she did tell Sid, "I'm glad you're helping with the cleanup because Gretchen is a total slob. Maybe she won't be so lazy with you around."

That was pretty good behavior for her, Gretchen thought.

"Mr. Simkin left us a mess in there," Mrs. Page said. "He was supposed to clean the garage out before we moved in, but he didn't. Feel free to throw everything out." She pointed out the kitchen window. "See? I rented a dumpster for all the junk. Just toss everything that's not worth keeping in there."

"Think there's anything valuable in there?" Sid asked.

She rolled her eyes. "Mr. Simkin showed us his collection of bottle caps. I think that was the most valuable thing he had."

She squinted at Sid over her coffee cup, as if seeing him for the first time. "What are *your* favorite subjects in school?"

Sid shrugged. "The usual."

"Are you going to college?"

"Probably," Sid replied.

She tapped a fingernail against the coffee cup. "Like one-word answers?"

"Yes," he said.

Mrs. Page didn't laugh. She made a shooing motion with her free hand. "There's stacks of old rusted tools in there. Try not to injure yourselves. No open wounds. I don't have insurance yet."

"That's cheery, Mom," Gretchen said. She led the way out the back door to the garage.

Sid banged a rhythm on the side of the big metal dumpster in the driveway. "Your mom is funny," he said.

"Ha-ha."

They stopped in the open doorway of the garage and peered inside. It was a two-car garage, concrete walls, a small dust-covered window on one side letting a square of pale afternoon sunlight wash in.

Gretchen's eyes swept over a long, coiled garden hose, rakes and brooms, a hand lawn mower, a big unopened bag of fertilizer, and boxes of gardening equipment against the wall to her left. A bike with both tires missing hung on the back wall next to some kind of rubber raft and a torn kite with no string.

Gretchen pointed to a tall stack of cartons against the other wall. "Let's start with those boxes. You pull them down, and I'll go through them."

"We'll *both* go through them," Sid said, squeezing her shoulder. "That's the fun part."

Gretchen pinched her nose. "What's that sour smell?"

Sid sniffed a few times. "Maybe a dead mouse behind the cartons. Or a dead raccoon or something."

"Oh, yuck."

Sid snickered. "This is Fear Street, remember? Could be a rotting corpse!"

"You're not funny," Gretchen said, trying not to inhale. "What's the big fuss about Fear Street, anyway?"

Sid hoisted a large cardboard carton down from the top of the stack. "Hasn't anyone told you about this street? About the Fear family? All the twisted, freaky things that happen here?"

Gretchen shook her head. "You mean for real?"

"For real. I can tell you some of it later." He grinned. "But I don't want to scare you away."

"Oooh, I'm shaking!" Gretchen said sarcastically.

Working together, they pulled open the first carton. It was filled with rusted ice skates, several pairs. Sid picked up the box, carried it to the driveway, and heaved it into the dumpster with a loud crash.

The kitchen window slid open. Mrs. Page stuck her head out. "Keep it down, okay?"

"Sorry." Sid turned and trotted back to the garage.

The second carton contained ragged bath towels, many of them with large brown stains. They were neatly folded and smelled of mildew. That carton went into the dumpster. The next carton held a tall stack of *Popular Mechanics* magazines. The magazine on top was dated June, 1986.

"Too bad he didn't save comic books," Sid said. "Those could be valuable."

Gretchen wiped a smudge of dirt off her forehead with the back of one hand. Despite the coolness of the late October afternoon, it was becoming hot in the garage.

They worked steadily, pulling down cartons from

several stacks lined against the wall. It became obvious that Mr. Simkin hadn't left anything of value behind. So far, everything they looked at had ended up in the dumpster.

Gretchen checked her phone. "We've been working an hour and a half," she said. "Want to take a break?"

Sid wiped his hands on the front of his sweatshirt. "Let's just deal with this bookshelf over here." He stepped up to a wide wooden bookshelf. All the shelves were missing except for the bottom one. A stringless fishing rod lay on the shelf and several coffee cans that might have been used for bait.

Sid bent to examine the cans, then stopped. "Weird," he muttered.

"What's weird?" Gretchen stepped up behind him.

"I think I recognize this. Isn't this your backpack?"

Gretchen studied it. "Yes. Yes, it is. How'd it get out here?"

Sid bent down and lifted it from the garage floor. "It's empty," he reported. "Oh no. Wait. What *is* this?"

Gretchen stared at it in his hand. A brown glass jar. The size of a mayonnaise jar. "What is it?"

Sid let the backpack fall to the floor. He turned the jar between his hands. A printed label came into view. "Oh, wow," he murmured. His eyes went wide. "Oh, wow."

"What?" Gretchen demanded, grabbing his arm. "Let me see it. What is it?"

He turned the jar so she could read the label:

SULPHURIC ACID.

"This is what they found on Madison's violin," he said. "This is what killed Madison." His hand trembled as he brought the brown jar closer. Then he raised his eyes to Gretchen. "It's half–empty. Gretchen . . . what did you *do*?"

34.

retchen uttered a cry. "Huh? You don't think I killed Madison—*do* you?"

Sid didn't answer. His eyes remained on the acid jar trembling in his hand.

"I-I-I . . ." Gretchen stammered. Sid's sudden betrayal made her go speechless.

"Hidden in the garage . . . In your backpack. . . ." Sid murmured, his voice just above a whisper. He kept blinking, as if he was trying to force the bottle out of his sight.

"Well, I didn't put it there!" Gretchen screamed, finding her voice. "Don't be a jerk, Sid. You know Madison was my friend. The only friend I've made here in Shadyside. Why would I kill her? Why?"

He shook his head. "I don't know. I . . . don't understand."

Gretchen pointed a trembling finger at the jar. "Put it down. Put it down, Sid. The police will be looking for fingerprints. Now they'll find your prints all over it."

Sid dropped the jar back into the backpack. He set the backpack down carefully. "I'm sorry, but—"

"I can't believe you thought that acid was mine," Gretchen said, feeling the anger tighten her chest. She crossed her arms in front of her. "Someone put it there."

"But when did you notice your backpack was gone?"

"I . . . I don't know." *Why was he questioning her? Shouldn't he be helping her? Supporting her?*

"But if I killed Madison and had half a bottle of acid left over, I wouldn't put it there," she said. "I wouldn't put it in my backpack and hide it in the front of the garage where anyone could find it. Do you think I'm stupid?"

Sid shook his head but didn't answer. He couldn't hide his confusion. His eyebrows were knitted tightly and his eyes kept darting from side to side, as if his thoughts were overloading him.

"Trust me," Gretchen continued. "If the acid was mine, I would have dumped it in a trash can as far away from my house as you can get." She gave Sid's shoulder a shove. "Think about it. Someone put that here. Someone who wanted it to be found in my garage."

Sid swallowed. "First someone took your backpack? Then they hid it in your garage with the acid in it?"

"You don't think Devra is capable of that?" Gretchen demanded.

"Yeah . . . I guess." He shook his head. "I'm sorry, Gretchen. I didn't mean to accuse you. I was just so shocked. I lost it for a moment."

Gretchen stared at the backpack, gritting her teeth. "Devra put it there. I know she did. She knew no one would believe that I killed Madison. She put it there as a warning, Sid. Don't you see? This is a warning of what she can do."

"But you have no proof—" Sid started.

"I told you," Gretchen interrupted him. "The night before she was killed, Madison said she had something important to tell me. Something she was *desperate* to tell me. Then, before she had a chance, she was murdered."

"I know. I remember. And you think Madison was desperate to tell you something about Devra."

"I'm sure she was, Sid. And I'm sure Devra murdered her to keep her from telling what she found out."

Sid shook his head. "But there's no way to prove it. No way—"

"Yes, there is," Gretchen said. She grabbed his hand and tugged him out of the garage. "We're going to prove it. At least, *almost* prove it. Let's go." She pulled him to the car, which her mother had parked halfway up the drive.

Sid still had his face twisted in confusion. "Where are we going?"

"To Devra's house. And let's hope she isn't home."

35.

Gretchen took Park Drive through town to North Hills, the wealthy section of Shadyside where Devra lived. Sid sat tensely beside her as she lurched through Saturday afternoon traffic.

"She lives on Heather Court," Sid announced. "It's a right turn off Park. You could have taken that shortcut." He pointed out his window.

"I'm new here, remember?" Gretchen snapped. "I don't know the shortcuts. How do you know where Devra lives?"

"I've been to her house," Sid said. "Some kind of school thing. It's a total mansion. I mean, you could fit your house in their ballroom."

"Huh? They have a ballroom?"

He nodded. "They have a pool table in it. And foosball and an awesome air hockey table. It's like an enormous game room."

She stopped at a light, turned, and squinted at him suspiciously. "You know an awful lot about her house."

"I know even more," Sid said. "It's Saturday afternoon, right? Devra has horseback riding lessons every Saturday."

The traffic started to move again. "You and Devra are a lot closer than I thought," Gretchen said, only half-seriously. "How do you know about her lessons?"

"My cousin Ernie works at the stable."

As they entered North Hills, the houses were larger, the front lawns wider and deeper. Tall hedges along the street hid many houses from view.

A team of gardeners was raking the dead leaves off a lawn as they turned onto Heather Court. A group of five or six small kids, shouting and laughing, chased after a soccer ball in the yard next door.

"Do you mind telling me what we're doing?" Sid asked. "Why exactly are we going to Devra's house when we know she isn't there?"

"I hope no one is there," Gretchen said. She slowed the car as the soccer ball bounced into the street. The kids waited at the curb for her to pass before running out to retrieve it.

"It's two blocks down," Sid said. "So? What are we doing?"

"Snooping," Gretchen answered.

Sid stared at her, waiting for her to say more.

"I have an idea," she continued finally. "About the

acid. Devra said she was using acid to remove the paint on the old cabinet she wanted to give her dad. And I think she used that acid to kill Madison. And then she planted it in my garage."

"I *know* that's your theory," Sid said impatiently.

"So what if we sneak into Devra's house, find the cabinet she was working on—and there's no acid anywhere around? Wouldn't that prove that she took the acid and put it in my garage?"

"Not really," Sid said. "Maybe she used the acid and removed the paint. And when she was finished with the acid, she threw it away."

Gretchen shook her head. "People don't just throw away acid. It's too dangerous."

Sid thought about it for a while, scrunching up his face in concentration. "They have servants who could get rid of the acid. Your idea is a bit crazy, Gretchen."

"It's not crazy," Gretchen insisted. She swerved to avoid a large pothole in the street. "Listen to me. When we get there and take a look, there won't be any acid bottle. Maybe it won't *totally* prove the one in my garage was the one Devra used. But it will *almost* prove it."

"What if there *is* an acid bottle there?" Sid said, frowning. "What will that prove?"

"That I'm wrong?" Gretchen replied, slowing at an intersection. "Why are you so eager to prove me wrong? It's like you're defending Devra."

"No way," Sid insisted. "I think Devra is horrible.

Ernie says she is the worst person in the world. She orders everyone around like they're her servants and complains when they're not fast enough for her. Ernie said she isn't even nice to the horses."

Gretchen edged the car into the next block. "Which house is it?"

Sid pointed. "The one with the tall hedge and the lampposts on both sides of the driveway. Park on the street. Don't pull into the driveway."

Gretchen rolled her eyes. "Do you think I'm an idiot? *Of course* I'm not going to pull into the driveway. We don't want to be seen—remember?"

"Okay, okay." Sid swept a hand tensely through his dark hair. "And your plan is?"

"First we have to see if Devra or her father are at home."

"What about servants?" Sid said, eyes on the tall house rising at the top of the tree-dotted lawn.

"Maybe they have Saturday off," Gretchen said. She pulled the car to a stop at the edge of the neighbor's lawn and cut the engine. "We'll start in the garage. Maybe she worked on the cabinet in there."

"And if it isn't there?" Sid demanded.

"We'll have to sneak into the house," Gretchen said, reaching for the car door handle.

Sid didn't move. "We're going to sneak into the house and look for what exactly? No acid bottle?"

Gretchen nodded. "If there's no acid bottle, Devra is a murderer. Trust me. I'm right."

"I . . . don't like this," Sid said, shaking his head.

She gave him a shove. "Let's get going. Get out of the car."

"Gretchen, what do we say if we get caught?"

"We'll think of something."

36.

Gretchen led the way to the driveway. They stopped in the shadow of the tall hedge. Gretchen wrapped her hands around one of the old-fashioned-looking lamp-posts and leaned forward, peering up the wide, gravel driveway.

The house stood at the top of a sloping lawn. A line of tall evergreen trees ran along the far edge of the prop-erty. Oak trees dotted the lawn, already winter bare. The grass had been raked. A tall mound of dead leaves leaned against one side of the house.

"The house is dark," Gretchen whispered. "That's a good sign."

Sid didn't reply. He had his hands shoved into his jeans pockets. His eyes glanced all around, revealing his ner-vousness.

"The garage is attached to the house," Gretchen re-ported. She shielded her eyes with one hand. "Wow. A three-car garage. The doors are closed." She turned to Sid, who lingered at the curb. "Are you with me or not?"

"I think you're crazy," he replied. "But I'm with you."

She motioned him forward. "If we keep in the shadow of the trees, it will be hard for anyone to see us."

Sid tapped her shoulder. "You don't think Mr. Dalby has a gun—do you?"

She pushed his hand away. "Now *you're* being stupid. He's not going to shoot us. If he sees us, he'll think we're friends of Devra's."

"Friends of Devra's snooping around in the garage."

Gretchen began trotting up the gravel drive, her shoes crunching loudly. "No sign of life, Sid. There's no one home. Let's hurry."

He hesitated another few seconds. Then he followed her, his eyes darting from side to side, his clenched fists still buried deep in his jeans pockets.

A gray squirrel, its jaws bulging with nuts, stood up straight in the center of the lawn and gazed at them as they jogged past. Its tail was raised behind it, and its eyes followed them warily as they made their way to the side of the garage.

Even though it was a short distance, Gretchen found herself breathing hard as she pressed herself against the brick wall at the side. She turned and did a quick survey of the windows of the house. No lights. No movement.

Feeling a little more confident, she slid around to the front of the garage and peered into the window of the first of the three doors. "Only one car in there," she reported to Sid. "At the other end. A convertible. I think it's a Jaguar."

"Sweet," Sid murmured.

Gretchen moved to the window on the middle door and pressed her face against the glass. She cupped her hands around the sides of her head to cut the glare of the sunlight behind them.

"Do you see a cabinet?" Sid stayed by the side wall. His eyes kept darting to the house.

"No. No cabinet," Gretchen reported. "Lots of shelves with gardening tools and supplies and other stuff. All very organized and neat."

"They probably have a garage servant who dusts the garage every day," Sid joked.

"Not funny." She turned to him. "Devra didn't work on the cabinet in here. We're going to have to get into the house."

Sid nodded. His expression went blank.

"They probably have a basement workshop," Gretchen said. "I'll bet that's where Devra worked on the cabinet." Keeping against the wall, she edged toward the entryway down a short passage from the garage.

Sid shook his head. "Maybe someday I'll write a book about two people who broke into a house to see if there was no acid bottle there."

"I didn't know you like to write," Gretchen said.

"I don't," Sid replied. "But I'll have to do *something* while I'm in prison for breaking and entering."

"Sssshh." Gretchen stepped down the five or six concrete steps that led to the door. She peered into the window. "Hey, this door leads right into the basement. We don't even have to go upstairs."

"Awesome," Sid whispered, brightening. "If we're real quiet . . ."

Gretchen tried the door knob. She turned it and pulled, and the door slid open. "Not locked. Come on. We got a break."

Sid took one last look around the backyard and side of the house. Then he slipped through the doorway after Gretchen.

"I don't hear any burglar alarm," Gretchen whispered. "Maybe we're okay."

They found themselves in a small, carpeted room. Gretchen saw a long counter obviously used as a desk, a laptop and printer, a small armchair, and a low vinyl couch. A tall bookshelf filled one wall. A framed photo of the Eiffel Tower in Paris was hung over the desk beside a wall calendar.

"It's like a little office," Gretchen said. She motioned for Sid to follow her as she stepped through a narrow, open doorway.

Gym equipment filled the next room. Gretchen saw a StairMaster machine, a stationary bike, an elliptical machine, a treadmill, several weights stacked on a shelf against the wall. A flatscreen TV was suspended on the wall facing the exercise machines.

"Wow. They've got *everything*," Sid whispered. "And it's just Devra and her dad?"

Gretchen didn't answer. She had her eyes on the low ceiling. She listened for footsteps or any other sounds above them, signs that someone was home.

Silence.

They both crept through the doorway on the far end of the gym. Orange sunlight through windows up at ground level revealed that this was the part that looked like a basement. No carpeting here. A massive furnace took up nearly half the room. Pipes and cables and rolls of insulation material, wooden crates, old furniture covered in bedsheets.

"I knew it. A workshop," Gretchen said, pointing. A long workbench stood against one wall with wooden shelves above it, a huge metal vice attached to one end. As she moved toward it, she saw a large power saw resting on a separate table. Small chunks of wood sat in a puddle of sawdust, littering the floor.

"There it is," Sid whispered, grabbing her shoulder. "You were right. That has to be the cabinet."

Gretchen followed his gaze. There it was, a small wooden cabinet with six drawers across the front. It was about the size of a bed table. Each drawer had a brass knob in its center, newly polished. The top was framed by a carved wooden design that looked a little like ocean waves.

"She removed all the paint," Gretchen said. "Look.

She's already started to stain the cabinet with some kind of dark stain." Her eyes went to the shelves above the workbench. "So where's the acid she used to remove the paint?"

Sid stepped up to the workbench. He gazed at the shelves filled with tools and supplies. A large can of wood stain stood at the edge of the workbench, a paint-brush beside it.

"I don't see it," Gretchen said, turning and searching for another table that might hold the supplies Devra used. "Nope. No acid bottle. I think I was right, Sid. I think the acid she used is in my garage."

"You're wrong," Sid said. He reached onto the high-est shelf and pulled something down. He turned and showed it to her.

Gretchen gasped. An orange bottle, a little larger than the one in her garage. She squinted hard at it. "Is it—?"

"It's an acid bottle," Sid said. "And it's almost empty. You were wrong, Gretchen. This is what Devra used. The acid in your garage—"

"Let me see it." She grabbed the bottle from his hand. She turned it so she could read the label. She raised it closer to her face and read the label out loud. "Muriatic Acid."

She and Sid stared at each other.

"What's Muriatic acid?" Gretchen whispered.

Sid shrugged.

Gretchen fumbled in her pocket and pulled out her

phone. Her fingers trembled as she brought up the Google app and typed in Muriatic Acid.

"It's an acid used to remove paint," she read it to Sid. "It's usually used to remove paint from cars. But it also works on furniture."

Her shoulders slumped. She suddenly felt as if she was deflating, like a balloon emptying out. "Oh, wow."

Sid placed the bottle of acid back on the shelf. "Have we proved anything here?"

Gretchen shook her head. "I don't think so. I . . . I don't know *what* to think, Sid. Now I'm totally confused. The acid in my garage . . . sulfuric acid. . . . That's the acid that killed Madison. And . . . and . . ."

They both heard the car door slam. They froze and listened. The hum of a garage door lowering itself. And then . . . the thud and bump of the basement door being pushed open.

Soft footsteps.

Gretchen gasped. "We're caught."

37.

While Gretchen and Sid were sneaking into the Dalby basement, Devra Dalby was across town, at Shadyside General Hospital. She came to visit her cheerleader friend Stacy. She had come straight from the stables and made quite an image and she walked in wearing her expensive riding outfit.

She arrived to the wail of ambulance sirens and the tense shouts of orderlies in pale green scrubs, who were rushing to the parking lot. The flashing blue-and-red lights reflected in her windshield as she maneuvered her Acura around the cluster of ambulances.

Devra slowed to let a wheeled stretcher go past. She slid down the window. "What happened?"

"Collision on Division Street," a young nurse answered, running beside the stretcher. "Three cars."

The entrance to the main parking lot was blocked, so Devra made her way to the lot in back of the big red-brick building. *Why do they have to block the entire lot?*

227

Why can't they park the ambulances by the emergency room door?

Devra always felt tense, jumpy, after a horseback riding session. The adrenaline rush stayed with her a long time. Horses, she felt, were smelly and stupid. But the rush of taking them from a trot to a full gallop was *outstanding*.

Mopping perspiration from her forehead with a tissue, she climbed out of the car. *I probably smell like a horse, but Stacy won't care. I'm sure she's bored to tears in there, desperate for visitors.*

The sirens had cut off, but the red-and-blue lights continued to flash. A hush fell over the parking lot as the hospital crew hurried to unload the injured from the ambulances.

Devra turned her head away as she walked. She didn't want to see any injured people. She took a certain pride in avoiding ugly things. Sure, she was squeamish, but wasn't that a good quality? Didn't that mean she was especially sensitive?

She stepped into the crowded reception area of the hospital and fumbled in her bag for her sunglasses. Why did the lighting in hospitals have to be so harsh? Wouldn't it be more comforting to patients to have the lights dim?

The woman in the reception booth was on the phone. Devra snickered. The woman was so fat, she nearly filled the whole booth. She ignored Devra, kept her eyes down as she talked.

Devra tapped her fingernails impatiently on the desktop. "Excuse me. I think you're supposed to help people."

The woman lowered her phone and glared at Devra. "I *am* helping someone."

Devra ignored her reply. "I need the room number of Stacy Grande. If it isn't too much trouble."

Muttering under her breath, the woman found the room number for Devra.

After an endless wait for an elevator, Devra found herself at the doorway to Stacy's room. She peeked in and saw that Courtney was already there, seated on a folding chair beside Stacy's bed.

Courtney jumped to her feet. "Devra! You're here!" She motioned with both hands. "Come see how great Stacy looks."

Devra stepped into the room and turned to Stacy in her bed. She didn't look great. She looked pale and thin, her hair a tangled mess, and tubes in both arms, heavy bandages over both arms and her hands.

"Hey," Devra said weakly, feeling her stomach lurch. "Stacy . . . How's it going?"

"Not so bad," Stacy said.

She's always so bright and perky. Even in a hospital bed covered in bandages.

"I'd hug you," Devra said, "But I don't think I can."

Stacy sighed. "The only hugs I get are when the nurses come to lift me out of bed."

"It's a cheerleader reunion," Courtney said, grinning at Devra. "We could have a spirit rally right here."

"Go, Tigers," Stacy said. Her voice was muffled. She didn't appear to Devra to have much strength.

"Someone should bring you some blusher or something," Devra blurted out.

Stacy blinked. "Am I *that* pale?"

Courtney laughed. "Devra, you're always so tactful." She pulled a folding chair to the other side of Stacy's bed and motioned for Devra to sit down.

"I can't stay long," Devra said. "I just came from the stable, and I'm a smelly mess." She dropped into the chair and gently wrapped a hand around Stacy's bandaged wrist. "So? What's the report?"

"I've got full movement in my hands," Stacy answered. "That's the good news. And the bad news? My chest is taking a long time to heal. The burn wounds are still pretty bad."

"Before you came we were just talking about how she's lucky in one way," Courtney said.

Devra squinted at Stacy. "Lucky?"

"Yes. The flames didn't reach my face. My face isn't burned or scarred at all."

Devra nodded. "You're right. That part is lucky." She leaned closer to Stacy. "I just feel so bad. Guilty."

Stacy blinked. "Guilty?"

"Well . . . I was supposed to take that fire baton,"

Devra said. "If I didn't suddenly have that stomach cramp, it would have been me. Not you."

"Well you can't feel guilty about *that*," Courtney chimed in. "You had no way of knowing."

Devra suddenly felt eager to change the subject. She had said what she came to say. Now she'd really like to get out of there. The hospital smell was making her nauseous. And she really didn't want to think about what Stacy's arms and chest looked like under all those bandages.

"Are your parents around?" she asked.

Stacy shook her head. "No. They were here this morning. But now they're at a lawyer's."

"Lawyers?"

"They're going to sue the school," Stacy said. "The lawyer thinks we can collect damages. If we sue them for negligence, I guess."

Devra shook her head. "Your parents should sue Gretchen Page. She's the one who was negligent."

"What's up with Gretchen?" Stacy asked. "She's the only one on the squad who hasn't come to visit me."

"Probably feels guilty," Courtney said.

"She *is* guilty," Devra said heatedly. "She did this to you, Stacy. Of course, I was supposed to go first. So I guess she wanted to burn *me*."

Stacy gasped. "You can't think it was deliberate, Devra. No way. It was a total accident. I'm sure of it."

"Why are you sure of it?" Devra demanded.

Stacy opened her mouth but didn't reply.

"Gretchen was so desperate to be on the squad," Devra continued. "She felt that I cheated her out of her place. So . . . if she handed me a baton soaked in kerosene, she could accomplish two things. Get rid of me and get her place on the squad."

"That's crazy," Courtney chimed in. "I'm sorry, Devra. I don't like Gretchen, either. But *no one* would try to burn someone up just to get on a cheerleader squad. No way. No way."

"She'd have to be a total psycho," Stacy said.

Devra jumped to her feet. "Well, who says she isn't? Who says she isn't a total psycho? Let's talk about Madison Grossman. Madison tried to be Gretchen's friend. As far as I know, she was Gretchen's only friend. And she ends up with acid burning through her neck and killing her."

Devra was breathless now, her voice high and shrill. She gave her red hair a violent toss behind her shoulders. "You get doused in kerosene and Madison is murdered with acid. You don't think there's a connection? The connection is Gretchen. Do you seriously think I'm just being paranoid?"

"Yes," both girls answered at once.

"Yes, you're being paranoid," Stacy said. "You have no reason to accuse Gretchen . . . no reason at all."

Devra's face was bright red and she was breathing hard, her chest heaving. "I have a real problem with Gretchen Page," she said, lowering her voice to a whisper. "I have to deal with Gretchen. I just haven't figured out how."

38.

Trapped in Devra's basement, Gretchen and Sid froze in panic. They heard the basement door click shut and the soft thud of approaching footsteps.

Gretchen turned to Sid. They both stood still, their bodies locked tight, waiting for their brains to unfreeze.

Nowhere to hide.

Sid dropped to his knees and squeezed under the worktable. But he was still in plain sight. Gretchen looked one way, then the other. The basement became a blur of grays and dark browns in her eyes.

The footsteps grew louder. Heavier.

This was stupid. We shouldn't be here. I didn't even prove anything about the acid.

Finally she dove behind Devra's wooden cabinet and dropped to her knees. She knew she was only half-hidden. But there was nowhere else. . . .

And then there he was, entering from the gym

doorway. A tall man in a dark suit, white shirt open at the collar. Gretchen could see him so clearly . . . *too* clearly. It meant he could see her.

If he turned to the left, he would see both her and Sid.

Her nose suddenly itched. *Oh no. Don't sneeze. This isn't a sitcom. This isn't a comedy. This is serious trouble. Don't sneeze.*

The man carried a black briefcase in one hand. He took long strides across the concrete basement floor. He had wavy dark hair, balding in front. A short mustache. Dark eyes behind owlish glasses.

He's so close to me now. He could almost reach out and touch me.

Devra's dad. It has to be Mr. Dalby.

He had been walking quickly toward the stairs that led to the first floor. But now he stopped.

Gretchen's heart stopped, too.

He senses something. Why did he stop? He knows someone is here. He can feel it.

Her panic was almost too much to bear. She almost let out a frightened scream.

We're caught. Caught. And no way to explain why we are here.

She had been holding her breath, struggling to hold back her sneeze. But now her chest felt about to burst.

And then a voice from the gym doorway. "Dad? Are you home? I saw your car."

Mr. Dalby spun around as Devra came walking into the basement. "I just got home," he said. "Where've you been?"

"It's Saturday, Dad. What do I do every Saturday?"

"Oh. Right. You were at the stable."

"Then I went to visit Stacy at the hospital."

He slid an arm around her shoulder, and they began to walk side by side to the stairs. Past Gretchen and Sid. Past them without seeing them.

"How is Stacy doing?" Mr. Dalby asked.

"She looks terrible" Devra said. "But everyone tells her she's doing really well."

"Such a tragedy," her dad murmured. "A tragedy."

"I guess she'll be okay eventually," Devra said. "She'll just have to cover up her arms for the rest of her life. And forget about wearing a bikini."

They disappeared up the stairs.

Gretchen and Sid didn't move. They didn't speak.

The upstairs door closed with a soft click. They could hear footsteps on the ceiling above them. They still didn't move.

Finally, Gretchen pulled herself upright behind the cabinet. "A close one," she whispered. Her whole body shuddered. Her skin tingled with lingering fear.

Sid scrambled out from under the workbench. "We're not out of here yet," he whispered.

Gretchen motioned for him to follow her. They both began to tiptoe toward the door to the garage. They were almost to the gym when a voice shouted, "HEY—WAIT!"

39.

A low cry escaped Gretchen's throat. She felt her knees start to fold. Sid grabbed her arm, his eyes wide with fright.

"Wait—" Devra's voice from the top of the stairs. "Dad, I left all my riding gear in the car. I'll be right back." She started down the steps.

Now we're trapped, Gretchen thought. *Now we're definitely doomed.*

"Get it later," Gretchen heard Mr. Dalby shout. "Come here. I want to show you something."

Gretchen held her breath until Devra had vanished from the stairway. "I guess that's what you call a close one," she whispered to Sid. She and Sid lurched out of the house and, keeping in the shadows as best they could, made their way, still shaking, still breathless, to her car.

"Did you pack any bug spray?" Mrs. Page asked, eyeing Gretchen's travel bag.

Gretchen rolled her eyes. "Mom, it's almost November, remember? I don't think bugs are going to be a problem."

"Spiders live into the winter," her mom said. "Especially in those camp cabins. They're probably infested with spiders."

"Well, thanks for giving me something to worry about once again," Gretchen said sarcastically. "I promise I won't go barefoot, okay?" She lifted the bag and started to the front door. The bag was heavier than she thought.

"Aren't you going to mention snakes?" Gretchen said. "The cabins are probably infested with snakes, too. There are probably snakes in every bed."

"You're so funny," Mrs. Page said, frowning. "Why do you get so much pleasure out of making fun of me?"

"Because it's so easy?"

"Any time I show a little concern, Gretchen, you ridicule me. Shouldn't you think about that?"

Gretchen set the bag down. "You don't show concern, Mom. You just try to create anxiety. You either try to put me down, or you tell me why I shouldn't do something I want to do. Shouldn't you think about *that*?"

Mrs. Page shook her head hard, as if shaking off Gretchen's words. "I don't understand why you have a cheerleader retreat in the middle of the school year. Especially with all the horrible things that have happened."

"I guess it's kind of for healing," Gretchen answered.

"Coach Walker thought we should keep the retreat, and spend some time together. Time to talk about things and just . . . get our heads together. And, I guess we'll concentrate on some new routines."

Mrs. Page didn't seem to hear her. "Did you remember to pack a hat?"

"Yes, Mom."

"I know it's not summer, but the sun is still strong. And with your fair skin—"

"I probably won't be able to call," Gretchen said. "Coach Walker warned us that there's practically no cell service in the woods, and the camp doesn't have WiFi."

"What if I need to reach you?"

Gretchen shrugged. "It's only four days."

"But . . . what if there's an emergency? I'm sure the school has made a plan for communicating in case there's some kind of emergency in the woods."

Gretchen uttered a disgusted groan. "See? There you go again. Worrying about nothing. Creating anxiety."

She suddenly pictured Devra.

Maybe I should be worried. Maybe Devra does have a plan for me, a plan to create an emergency.

A shiver of fear ran down her body. She hoped her mother couldn't see it. She never wanted her mother to see her being the tiniest bit fearful. That would give her mom too big a victory.

A horn honked out at the street.

"I've got to go," Gretchen said. "That's the bus that's

taking us to the campground." She set down her bag to open the front door.

Mrs. Page stepped up behind her. "Don't I at least get a hug? I won't see you for four days."

Gretchen turned and obediently hugged her mother. She felt a stab of emotion. Her mother was a difficult person. No. An impossible person. But Gretchen realized she still loved her. She still needed her.

"Have a good time, dear," Mrs. Page said, forcing a smile.

"I'll try," Gretchen said. And she carried her bag out the front door.

Mrs. Page carried her coffee mug into the den and sat down on the couch. *The Today Show* was on the TV, and they were showing a wildfire somewhere in California. She had the sound turned low. The TV was just a background blur to her thoughts.

The coffee was strong and bitter, the way she liked it. She found herself thinking about her ex-husband, Gretchen's father. She could never have strong coffee when he was around. It gave him heartburn, he said. *Now I can make it as strong as I like.* One of the advantages of being divorced.

Of course, one of the *disadvantages* was having to deal on her own with a teenage daughter. Gretchen had become so sarcastic and bitter. The move to Shadyside had given her a fresh start, a chance to make new friends and start her life all over again. Why was she so angry all the time?

And why does she take it out on me?

Yes, there had been some tragedies at the school. One girl burned so badly in a horrible accident. And another girl murdered in front of the whole school.

Did that explain Gretchen's attitude?

Gretchen's mom swept her hair back over her nightgown. *Time to get dressed.* The TV show had moved on to a scene of damaged buildings and crying people somewhere in the Middle East. The news was just unbearable these days.

She set down her coffee cup and clicked off the TV. Then she made her way upstairs, thinking about how Gretchen never liked the outdoors. *She even hated the day camp we sent her to.*

She stepped into Gretchen's room and gasped. Hurricane Gretchen had struck! The room looked as if it had been turned upside and everything from the closets and shelves and drawers flung everywhere.

The bedspread lay in a heap on the floor. Jeans and T-shirts littered the carpet. Her backpack lay open in a corner with notebooks and papers spilling out of it. A dresser drawer overflowing with black tights sat on the bed next to a pile of sweaters and sweatshirts.

I really don't believe this. She thinks of me as her servant. I'm just here to clean up after her.

Mrs. Page uttered a gasp when she spotted the phone

on top of the pile of sweaters. She picked it up and pushed it on. "Oh, wow," she murmured out loud. "Gretchen is *not* going to be happy. She left her phone behind."

And then . . . she couldn't help herself. She prided herself at not being a snoop. She had to keep watch on Gretchen. Had to act as a responsible parent. More than that, a caring parent. But she never wanted to be a snoop.

But here it was. And here she was, scanning through Gretchen's emails. Nothing interesting . . . nothing interesting at all.

But then Mrs. Page checked out the phone log. She glanced through the recent calls. Squinted hard at the calls Gretchen had made *because she didn't want to see what she was seeing on the screen.*

She didn't want to see these calls. She wanted them to vanish. This was the *last* thing she wanted to see.

And then, she couldn't help herself. She felt the tears run down her cheeks. And she started to murmur in a trembling whisper: "Oh no . . . Oh, please . . . Oh, no."

40.

She knew she had to act, but her brain wouldn't cooperate. The room spun. *I'm not even dressed. I haven't brushed my hair.*

Her first instinct was to drive to school, maybe catch the bus before it left for the woods or wherever it was going. But no. By the time she got dressed . . .

She spun away from Gretchen's room. She strode unsteadily into her room and picked up the phone on the bed table.

How do I reach the school? I don't know the number? Is there still Information, or has the Internet ended that?

She pushed 411 with a trembling finger. One ring . . . two . . .

She brushed the tears off her cheeks. "Can you connect me with Shadyside High School? It's kind of an emergency."

She was transferred to another operator. Then cut off.

Then heard the phone ringing at the high school on her next try.

"I need to speak to the principal. What's his name? Hernandez?"

"Who's calling, please?"

"It's Eleanor Page. I'm Gretchen Page's mother. I really need to speak to the principal."

"Can I put you on hold? I need to see if he's in his office."

"Okay. Okay. But, please—"

A *click*. Then silence.

She tapped her fingers on the bed table. Wrapped the phone cord around her wrist as she waited. And waited.

Finally, a man's voice. "Hello? This is Victor Hernandez."

"The principal?" Her voice came out hoarse. She coughed and cleared her throat. "Mr. Hernandez?" She shut her eyes, trying to steady herself, slow herself down, get her thoughts in order.

"Yes. Can I help you?"

"This is Gretchen Page's mother."

"Oh, yes. Hello, Mrs. Page. How are you?"

"Has the bus taking the cheerleaders to the retreat . . . has it l–left?" she stammered. "I really hope—"

"Yes. It's on its way to the campgrounds," Hernandez replied. "Coach Walker reported everyone is onboard. Do you need to speak to your daughter? Did she forget to bring something?"

"N–no, I don't need to speak to Gretchen. I need to speak to *you*."

"Well . . . if there's a problem . . ."

"I'll be right there," Mrs. Page said. "I'll be right there. I have to see you right away."

Gretchen pawed through her clothing. Some shirts toppled out of the bag and fell over the seat beside her. She reached the bottom of the bag, her hand grappling at the smooth leather.

"Gretchen—what are you doing?" Shannon stood in the bus aisle, leaning over Gretchen. She picked up a sweatshirt that had fallen into the aisle and handed it to her. "Did you lose something?"

Gretchen let out a growl. "Yeah. My phone. I think I left it at home." She started furiously stuffing her clothes back into the travel bag.

The bus hit a bump and several girls cried out. The bag jumped in Gretchen's lap.

"Maybe your mom can FedEx it to you," Shannon suggested.

"I can picture it. I know where I left it," Gretchen said. She slapped her forehead. "How could I be so dumb?"

Coach Walker edged up beside Shannon. "Don't worry about it, Gretchen," she said, eyeing the tangle of clothes on the seat. "I told you girls your phones will probably be worthless at the camp. There is no service up there. No cells for miles."

Gretchen gritted her teeth. "I just hate being forgetful."

Shannon helped her shove all her belongings back into the bag, and she hoisted it back onto the overhead rack. Flat, gray farmland whirred past outside the bus window. The fields were bare. The low clouds that appeared to be following the bus shut out any sunlight and made it look like the middle of winter outside.

Shannon motioned to the back of the bus. "Check out Sid. The only guy on this trip. He gets his own cabin. And he has all six of us to flirt with him. Is he a happy dude or what?"

Gretchen turned and followed Shannon's gaze. No. Actually Sid didn't look happy at all. He was in the very backseat, squeezed next to Devra. They were both talking at once, gesturing with their hands.

Squinting down the bus aisle into the gray light, it took Gretchen a while to realize they were shouting at each other, their expressions cold and angry.

Holding onto the seatback in front of her, Gretchen kept her eyes on them, watched their angry gestures. She couldn't hear what they were saying over the roar and rumble of the bus, but she could see they were practically spitting their words at each other.

Ducking her head so they wouldn't see her watching them, she was suddenly filled with confusion and surprise.

What on earth are Sid and Devra fighting about?

41.

Mrs. Page emptied out her pocketbook into the plastic tray and shoved the tray at the security guard, a lanky black woman wearing a loose-fitting blue uniform and a Chicago Cubs cap over her hair. A plastic name badge said her name was Audrey.

"In my day, we didn't have to go through a metal detector to get into school," Mrs. Page said.

"It's a different world, ma'am," Audrey replied.

Mrs. Page gazed down the long empty hall, yellow tile walls, gray metal lockers lining both sides. She heard a steady thumping sound and saw a boy two-thirds of the way to the end slowly dribbling a basketball on the floor as he walked. A maroon-and-white banner strung from the ceiling read: TIGERS ROAR.

"Do I have to remove my watch?" she asked the guard.

Audrey shook her head. "No. You can go right through. Just sign in." She shoved a long clipboard toward Mrs. Page.

She scribbled her name on the sign-in sheet. Audrey studied the signature. "Oh. Are you Gretchen's mother? She's the cheerleader, right? Very nice girl. Always says good morning."

"I'm kind of in a hurry," Mrs. Page, shoving her stuff back into her pocketbook. "I've never been here. Which way is the principal's office?"

Audrey pointed. "Make a left, then a right."

Mrs. Page turned and started to hurry away.

"Your top is buttoned crooked," Audrey called after her.

"Huh?" She lowered her gaze to the front of her pale green blouse. She saw immediately that the two sides didn't meet. She had the buttons in the wrong button holes. No time to fix it.

A few seconds later, she burst into the principal's office. The secretary behind the front desk looked up from a folder she had been reading. "Can I help you?"

"I need to see Mr. Hernandez right away." Mrs. Page saw the door to the inner office and strode toward it without waiting for the woman's reply.

"He has someone in there—"

She lurched into the doorway. Hernandez, behind the desk, was tall and broad, nearly bursting out of a gray suit, shirt unbuttoned, dark-framed glasses over his eyes.

He looks more like a gym teacher than a principal, she thought.

Two students, both blond, a boy and a girl, sat in chairs facing the desk.

All three of them looked up in surprise as Mrs. Page stepped in.

"I need to talk to you right away." She couldn't keep her voice from trembling. One hand went to her throat as if to be as dramatic as possible.

He squinted at her. "Are you Gretchen's mother?"

She nodded.

He turned to the two kids. "Let's continue our talk after lunch. Can you come back sixth period?"

They both nodded and scurried out without a word.

Hernandez motioned to a seat, but Mrs. Page remained standing. "You look upset. Is there a problem?"

She nodded. "I-I don't know where to start," she stammered. She changed her mind and slid into one of the chairs."

"It's about Gretchen?"

"Yes. Of course." She clasped her hands tightly in her lap. "I thought she was doing well. I thought she was okay. . . ." Her voice trailed off.

Hernandez removed his glasses. Pinched the brim of his nose. Replaced the glasses. Waited for her to continue, not taking his eyes off hers.

"She got on the bus for the retreat," Mrs. Page finally continued. "I went up to her room and I saw that she left her phone behind. I . . . I couldn't resist. I looked through it."

Hernandez leaned forward over the desktop. "You looked at her emails? Her Facebook?"

"Her phone calls," Gretchen mother replied. "I looked through her call log. I haven't done it for a long while. I . . . thought she was okay. But . . ."

She sucked in a deep breath. "But . . . I found all these calls. Gretchen was making calls almost every day . . . to a girl named Polly Brown."

Behind his glasses, Hernandez' eyes narrowed in concentration. "What's wrong with *that*, Mrs. Page?"

"Polly Brown has been dead for two years. Gretchen . . . Gretchen killed her."

42.

Hernandez uttered a sharp gasp. "Killed her?"

Mrs. Page grabbed her throat again. "I . . . shouldn't have said that. Gretchen was *responsible* for Polly's death. I mean, she didn't kill her deliberately. Polly was her best friend. They were inseparable. Closer than sisters. I—I—"

Gretchen's mother started to choke. Shaking her head, she held her throat and coughed.

"Miss Rangell," Hernandez shouted. "Please bring Mrs. Page a bottle of water."

Gretchen's mother heard scurrying in the outer office. She forced herself to swallow. Her throat suddenly felt dry as cotton. The secretary appeared with the bottle of water. Mrs. Page took several long sips.

"Better. Thank you." She smiled at the secretary, who disappeared back to the outer office.

Her smile faded as she turned back to the principal. "Gretchen and Polly were on their way to a basketball game. This was back in Savanna Mills. Gretchen was driving. She'd only had her license a few weeks, but she was a good driver, I think. Confident. Not nervous . . . like me."

She took another sip of water. "They were just a few blocks from the high school. I guess Gretchen was distracted. She was thinking about her cheerleading routines. She was the star . . . the best cheerleader at Savanna Mills. But . . ."

She stifled a sob. "Gretchen didn't see the van. She should have swerved or stopped or something. But she didn't see it. It . . . it . . ."

"Take your time," Hernandez said softly, his big hands spread over the desktop.

"It was a horrible head-on collision. Polly was reaching for something on the floor. She had her seatbelt open. She . . . she flew right through the windshield. She died before she landed. She didn't have a chance."

"Oh my goodness," Hernandez murmured, shaking his head. He lowered his eyes. "How horrible."

"Yes. Horrible," Mrs. Page repeated in a whisper.

Silence for a long moment.

Mrs. Page was the first to break the silence. "Gretchen was lost after that. I mean really lost. We . . . we couldn't get through to her. . . . Her father and I . . . we tried everything. We took her to all the best doctors. But . . ."

Another long pause.

"But we couldn't reach her. Couldn't get through to her. She was lost. Just lost. In her own world. No touch with reality." She raised her eyes to Hernandez. "She wouldn't talk to anyone. For weeks, she wouldn't get out of bed. She wouldn't eat. She . . . just tried to vanish from the world."

Hernandez swallowed. "Take your time, Mrs. Page. Tell me what happened next."

"The doctors brought her around," Gretchen's mother replied. "They found the right meds. They found the right approach. They brought her back. My marriage had broken up by then. The stress was just too much for her father and me. We couldn't handle it, and we divorced."

Hernandez shook his head. He lowered his gaze to the desktop.

"But when Gretchen started coming around, her father and I were overjoyed. We had our daughter back. And she . . . she seemed like her old self in every way."

Mrs. Rangell poked her head into the office. "Mr. Mulrooney from the State Education Board is on line one?"

Hernandez waved a hand. "Tell Anthony I'll have to call him back." He turned back to Mrs. Page. "And now you're worried—?"

"When Gretchen starts to call Polly, it means she's losing it again. Backing away from the real world.

2

Something starts to bother her . . . something starts to eat at her . . . and she starts to sink back. . . ."

"What do you think caused the problem?" Hernandez asked.

"I . . . I think maybe the cheerleading. I tried to discourage her. I tried to convince her to wait. To take it slow. It meant so much to her. But I shouldn't have let her join. I should have stopped her. I'm afraid she may be going back to her old pattern . . . to what she did back in Savanna Mills."

Hernandez leaned forward over the desk. "Her old pattern?"

"Back home, she picked out one girl. One girl on the cheerleading squad. And then Gretchen made herself look like a victim."

Hernandez squinted hard. "I don't understand."

"She made it look as if the girl was persecuting her. Harassing her. Doing terrible things to embarrass her. Gretchen tried to turn everyone against that girl, even though the girl wasn't doing *anything* to her. Gretchen did it all to *herself*."

"Oh no," Hernandez muttered. "Gretchen may be doing that again. Devra Dalby, one of the cheerleaders . . ."

"That's what I was afraid of," Mrs. Page said. "When I saw she was making calls to her dead friend, I thought maybe she could be starting the pattern all over again."

Hernandez swept a hand back through his dark hair.

"You should have told the school about your daughter's history," he said. "We don't have any of this in our records, and we really should know about it all."

Mrs. Page lowered her eyes but didn't reply. "I haven't told you the worst of it. I haven't told you about the knife."

Hernandez blinked. His mouth opened slightly. He waited for her to continue.

"When Gretchen was acting most paranoid . . . when she was accusing this girl at school of trying to harm her . . . we found a knife. Hidden at the bottom of her backpack. A hunting knife. Very long and very sharp."

She shuddered. "That was the low point. That was when I was most frightened. Of course, we took the knife away. And she never used it. . . . But we couldn't get Gretchen to talk about it. I tried. The doctors tried. She never said a word."

"Oh my God," Hernandez muttered. "So . . ." He took a breath. "So you think your daughter might be dangerous right now?"

Mrs. Page bit her lip. "I . . . I . . ."

Hernandez was breathing hard. "We've had one girl badly burned and another girl murdered in a most hideous and shocking way. A lot of tragedy for this school. A lot of sadness. Too much sadness for one school." His eyes were suddenly watery. They locked on hers. "You don't think Gretchen—?"

The unfinished question hung in the air.

Then, Mrs. Page spoke in a voice just above a whisper. "I think we have to get Gretchen away from those other cheerleaders as fast as we can."

43.

Gretchen never thought it would come to this.

Sure, there was tension on the bus that brought them to this campgrounds in the woods. More than tension. A long argument between Devra and Sid that soon became a screaming fight.

Coach Walker had to go to the back of the bus and break it up. She demanded to know what the problem was. But, of course, neither of them would speak up. Devra just stared back at Coach Walker, her face tight with disgust.

Sid sat beside Devra, his cheeks bright red and glistening with sweat. He kept his eyes lowered and wouldn't say a word.

Shaking her head, hands clenched into tight fists, Coach Walker returned to her seat at the front of the bus.

The tension between Sid and Devra simmered, but the shouting had stopped.

Gretchen kept twisting in her seat, taking peeks at

them. *What did Devra do to get Sid steamed like that?* She wondered. *He looks ready to explode.*

Sid had slid across the seat, away from Devra. He had his arms crossed tightly in front of him, his face still red. He stared out the window at the passing farm fields.

Devra pushed her earphones into her ears and fiddled with her phone. She blew a strand of red hair off her face and settled back in the seat. She appeared a lot calmer than Sid. And now they both ignored one another as if nothing had happened.

Shannon leaned across the bus aisle and said something to Gretchen. But Gretchen didn't hear her. She was thinking hard about the argument—the fight—in the back of the bus, struggling to guess what could have sparked it.

Was it about me?

And then the bus had come to a stop outside the rustic camp mess hall that looked like a big log cabin. Their bags were being unloaded, and Coach Walker, clipboard in hand, was assigning them to their cabins. One for Walker. One for Sid. Three girls each in the two small cabins on the other side of the mess hall.

Gretchen was put in a cabin with Shannon and Becka.

Did Coach Walker deliberately separate me from Devra?

Not enough time to unpack. They had to rush to their first squad meeting in the mess hall. Coach Walker always insisted on promptness.

The girls wore black tights or jeans and sweatshirts

and still hugged themselves for warmth. There was no heat in the big hall, and no one had started a fire yet in the enormous fireplace against the back wall.

And then the trouble ignited again. The screams and accusations.

And this time it got really bad.

Really bad.

Gretchen covered her ears and ran screaming from the mess hall. The afternoon sun sent shifting patterns on the grass, filtering through the tall trees. Shadows moved at her feet as she ran.

Ran breathlessly to her cabin. Her bag still propped on her bed, only half-unpacked.

Gretchen knew what she had to do.

Yes, her mind was spinning, flying, pictures danced and disappeared, the cabin now a dark swirl of grays and blacks.

But she knew what she had to do.

She had to put an end to it.

She could hear the cries from the mess hall.

She had to hurry.

With a choked cry, Gretchen dug her hand deep into her travel bag . . . slid it under the clothes . . . under her cosmetics bag.

She wrapped her fingers around the knife she had hidden there, lifted it out, the long blade dull in the dim cabin light.

I'm ready.

44.

Mrs. Page struggled to tighten her seatbelt as Mr. Hernandez swerved, guiding his Subaru SUV through traffic in the Old Village. "These streets are too narrow," he said, groaning. "They were too narrow when the town was built. And now they're ridiculous."

He roared the SUV onto the sidewalk to edge it around a slow-moving garbage truck. Mrs. Page bounced against the passenger seat.

"I'm so sorry," she said. "So sorry I didn't let the school know about Gretchen's problems. But she was doing so well. Her therapist felt that getting away to a new place was the right thing to do."

Hernandez nodded, peering through his sunglasses at the line of traffic in front of them. "I don't know if we'd have done anything differently," he said. "Maybe kept a closer eye on her. Listened to her complaints about Devra Dalby a little more seriously . . . ."

"How far are we from the camp?" she asked.

"Only about forty-five minutes. If traffic starts moving. We should be okay once we get past town."

They rode in silence for a while. The sun slid over the windshield, forcing Mrs. Page to shield her eyes.

"I'm sorry, but I need to ask," Hernandez said, frowning. "And there's no gentle way to ask it. Do you think Gretchen could have killed Madison Grossman? Wasn't Madison her friend?"

Mrs. Page pressed her hands together, fingers tightly entwined, almost as if praying. "I don't know. I really don't. I . . . I don't think my daughter is a murderer. She is a troubled girl. I mean . . . I can't picture her . . . I just can't imagine—" Her words broke off with a sob.

"Can you think of any reason at all she would have for murdering Madison Grossman?"

Mrs. Page shook her head. "No. No reason. Madison was her only new friend since moving here. At least, I *think* she was. You have to understand, Mr. Hernandez, Gretchen is very private. She doesn't confide in me." And then she added, as if an afterthought: "Oh. I think there was a boy, too."

Hernandez' eyes widened. "A boy?"

"Yes. I met him. Nice looking. Gretchen seemed to like him. I just got a vibe, a feeling. She didn't say they were going together or anything. He came to help her clean out the garage last Saturday."

"You don't remember his name?"

She shook her head. "I'm sorry. I don't. I was so

shocked that she seemed to have a boyfriend. . . ." Her voice trailed off again.

Hernandez hit the brake, nearly hitting the SUV in front of them. "Can you describe him?"

Mrs. Page thought for a while. "Well, he had one of those very trendy haircuts. Awful. You know. Buzzed very short on the sides and long on the top. Brown hair. And . . . I remember he had very big ears. He was nice looking, except for the big ears."

"Sounds like Sid Viviano," Hernandez said. "He's the equipment manager for the cheerleader squad."

"Yeah. Maybe," she said. "That would make sense, I guess."

"But everyone in school knows that Sid and Stacy Grande are a couple. Have been for a long time."

Mrs. Page didn't answer. She took a shuddering breath. "I thought I was paying close attention to Gretchen. She accused me of paying *too much* attention. But . . . I guess I didn't do my job. I should have been more responsible. I should have watched her even more closely."

They drove in silence for a while. The traffic eased as they left Shadyside. The afternoon sun began to dip, lowering itself over the flat gray and brown farms that ringed the town.

Mrs. Page kept her eyes shut. Hernandez knew she wasn't asleep. Was she praying?

He wondered if she had told him everything about Gretchen. He imagined there were big chunks of the story she had left out. He kept thinking about the knife they found in Gretchen's backpack. Thinking about it caused a hard rock to form in the pit of his stomach.

Dread made his entire body feel heavy as he swung the SUV into the dirt driveway to the campgrounds. Tall trees reached their limbs over the narrow drive, sending shadows over them, deepening as they followed the drive to the camp.

Mrs. Page's eyes snapped open. Her face locked in a wide-eyed expression of fear and anxiety. Spotty sunlight dappled the roofs of the line of small wooden cabins, abandoned this time of year.

The car sank into a deep hole in the dirt, then bounced back up, causing Mrs. Page to cry out.

Hernandez slowed the car as they passed two cabins with lights on, the pale light seeping from the small dirt-smeared windows. And then they could see at the end of the row of cabins a large two-story building that must be the mess hall.

A sudden movement along the path caught Mrs. Page's eye. She saw a girl running toward the mess hall entrance. And she gasped. "Is that Gretchen?"

Hernandez stopped the car as the girl neared the building door.

Yes. Yes. It was definitely Gretchen. Her blond hair flying behind her, gleaming dully in the late afternoon sun.

Yes it was Gretchen. And yes, that was a knife in her hand. A knife raised as if ready to attack.

"No. Oh no," Mrs. Page moaned.

She and Hernandez reached for the door handles, intending to leap out of the car and stop her.

Too late.

Gretchen vanished into the mess hall.

And instantly, they heard screams, shrill and frightened. High screams of terror ringing through the open windows. And the horrified shout of Coach Walker: "Stop! No—please! STOP!"

45.

Over the screams of the girls in the mess hall, Gretchen could hear the rapid thump of blood pulsing in her ears and feel the drumbeat of her heart in her chest. Fighting against her panic, she shoved open the mess hall door with her shoulder and burst into the long room.

She blinked. In her panic, her eyes were playing tricks on her. The room was suddenly bathed in red. Blood red. Everyone at the long table in the center of the room shimmering red, as if soaked in blood.

Blinking hard, she forced the real colors back, and as the blanket of red faded, she lurched toward them all, her eyes darting from one to the other. Their screams grew more shrill and desperate as she raised the knife. Waved it in front of her. Made sure that Sid saw the long blade.

Sid saw her. His eyes were wide with surprise.

He stood behind Devra with one arm around her chest, gripping her hard, holding her defenseless against him. And a knife in his other hand pressed against Devra's pale throat.

Devra's eyes rolled crazily. Her hair was wild about her face. She couldn't scream. The knife blade was too tight against her skin.

"Drop it, Sid!" Gretchen screamed in a trembling shrill voice she'd never heard before. "Drop the knife! Let Devra go—*now*!"

The other cheerleaders had jumped up from the table and backed away. They huddled against the wall.

Coach Walker stood frozen at the other end of the table, her arms stretched out helplessly, as if pleading with Sid, her face stuck in an open-mouthed expression of pain and shock.

Gretchen saw her mother burst into the room, followed by Principal Hernandez. *How did they know there was trouble?* They both froze at the door and didn't come any closer.

Gretchen took a step closer to Sid and Devra, waving the knife in her trembling hand. Her heart was beating so hard, she thought her chest might explode.

"Drop it, Sid," she repeated. "I'm serious. Let Devra go. I'll cut you. I'm not afraid. I'll cut you."

Sid pressed his knife blade against Devra's throat. "It was supposed to be Devra," he shouted, his voice ringing with anger. "It was supposed to be Devra—not Stacy. Devra was supposed to burn."

Gretchen gasped. "It was *you*, Sid? You deliberately poured the kerosene on the baton?"

"It was supposed to be Devra!" he screamed. "Not Stacy. I didn't want to burn Stacy. Devra was supposed to burn!" His voice cracked. He tightened his grip around Devra, who slumped as if defeated, sank against him, stopped struggling to escape.

Sid slid the blade against Devra's throat. Girls screamed as a thin trickle of bright blood appeared on her neck.

Devra let out a whispered moan. "Oh, please . . . It hurts. . . ."

"Don't do it! Don't cut her, Sid!" Gretchen cried. She took another step closer, gripping the knife handle so tightly her hand throbbed with pain.

I've got to keep him talking, Gretchen thought. *It's the only way. If I can keep him talking, maybe I can stop him from killing her.*

"Why, Sid? Why does Devra have to die?"

"She knows! She knows!" The words exploded from his mouth.

Blood trickled down Devra's neck. Sid kept the blade pressed against her skin.

Against the wall, Shannon and Ana were sobbing, their faces covered by their hands.

"I did everything . . . everything to ruin Devra. To make everyone hate her. I . . . I had to ruin her . . . the way she ruined my family."

Gretchen kept the knife poised. "What do you mean, Sid? What are you saying?"

"I . . . I did everything," Sid repeated. His eyes were glassy, seemed far away. He was in his own world now. Talking more to himself than to Gretchen and the others. "I stole her phone and sent those threatening text messages to you. I put the drain cleaner in your water bottle and stuffed the cockroaches in your new uniform. I . . . I put on Devra's perfume and attacked you in the gym. I had to ruin Devra. I had to show Devra I could be in charge. I had to pay her back. I wanted *everyone* to hate Devra as much as I do."

"But, why, Sid? Why?"

"She knows! She *knows*!" he screamed, eyes wild, face bright red now. "Devra and I . . . I thought we had a connection. We were going out. Stacy didn't know anything. Devra and I . . . I thought we had a good thing. I really did. I thought we had something real. And then . . ."

His jaw tightened. A low growl escaped his throat. He pressed the blade tighter against Devra's neck.

"Don't kill her! Sid—you don't want to kill her!" Coach Walker shouted, finally finding her voice.

"Why shouldn't I?" He spit the words at her. "She killed my family. She ruined my life. I thought Devra and I were close—really close—but then . . . then . . . My dad, he worked at Dalby's. In the shoe department.

He was a good salesman. And he was a loyal worker. He always talked about what a good department store it was and how he enjoyed his job."

He stopped, his chest heaving. He took a deep breath, as if it was too much for him to tell. His eyes were wild. They wouldn't rest on any spot. Large drops of sweat rolled down his forehead and cheeks.

"Devra had my dad fired," he finally continued his story, lowering his voice to nearly a whisper. "She reported him to the manager. She said he was rude to a customer, and she had him fired. We were going out, Devra and I. I thought we were serious. I thought it was a real thing. And she had my dad fired. Don't you see? I didn't mean *anything* to her. Nothing at all."

He jerked Devra hard, spinning her to the side.

"It broke my dad," he said, his voice cracking again. "My dad was never the same. And neither was my family. She ruined my family. Ruined everything. She was supposed to burn. Not Stacy. Not Stacy. Devra was supposed to burn."

"No!" Gretchen screamed. "Sid—don't!"

I've got to keep him talking. It's the only chance.

"What about Madison?" Gretchen cried. "Sid—what about Madison? Do you know who killed Madison?"

He blinked. "Who killed Madison? I did. I did, of course."

Gretchen gasped. Loud sobs rang out beneath the

low rafters. Gretchen's whole body tingled. The knife trembled in her hand. It wasn't the answer she had expected.

She liked Sid so much. And now she was learning she didn't know him at all. He was a murderer. A murderer. She trusted him. She opened herself to him. And he was a murderer.

"Why, Sid? Why did you kill her?"

"She had a video on her phone. She didn't even know she had it. But she found it. A video at the football game. It showed me wiping kerosene on the fire baton. It showed me. So clearly. Madison had the video. And she said she was taking it to Hernandez."

He nodded to the principal. Hernandez and Mrs. Page still hadn't moved. They stood frozen at the mess hall doorway.

A sob escaped Gretchen's throat. She nearly dropped the knife. "Oh my God, Sid. I don't believe . . . I just can't believe you killed Madison."

He sneered at her. "What choice did I have?" He jerked Devra hard again. "Was I supposed to let her show the video to Hernandez? To the police? Enough talk. Devra has to die now. *She* was supposed to burn—not Stacy. Not Stacy!"

His eyes rolled crazily in his head. Spit flew from his mouth with every word. "It was supposed to be Devra! Devra—not Stacy!"

"Let me go!" Devra found her voice. Her plea came out in a high-pitched shriek. "Let me go! Let me go!"

She made a sick gagging sound as Sid slowly slid the blade across her neck.

46.

Against the wall, girls screamed. Courtney dropped to her knees. Becka and Shannon hugged one another. Ana kept her hands covering her face.

Devra uttered a long groan. Sid loosened his hold on her, the knife still raised, and she sank to her knees.

Gretchen felt a surge of energy. The room went red again. Before she realized it, she was diving forward, stumbling, almost staggering toward Sid. She let out an angry roar, a cry like a hurt animal.

All that betrayal . . . all of the cruel jokes Sid had played on her . . . the cockroaches . . . the threatening texts . . . the acid in her garage . . . his lies . . . all the while, pretending to care about her.

Later, Gretchen would think about how she had been used, how he had entrapped her in his insane desire for revenge.

But now, she felt only fury, a fury that made the room go blood red, that pushed her forward, that forced her to scream like an enraged beast. She tossed away her knife, lowered her shoulder, and barreled into Sid.

He saw her coming, but he didn't react fast enough. She drove her elbow into his midsection, and the knife dropped from his hand. He groaned and tried to back away from her. But Gretchen drove a fist hard under his chin.

She heard a cracking sound—the sound of his neck breaking? His head snapped back. His eyes went wide, his mouth dropping open in pain and shock. He fell backward, fell hard, smashing the back of his head against the wooden table edge as he went down.

Sid crumpled to the floor, his legs splayed at an odd angle, his head tilted, eyes shut. Gretchen stood over him, every muscle tensed, breathing noisily, expecting him to climb to his feet.

But he didn't move.

She turned and saw that Devra had crawled to Coach Walker. Walker had wrapped a dish towel around Devra's throat. "She'll be okay," Walker shouted to everyone. "The cut isn't deep."

The other cheerleaders gathered around Devra and Coach Walker. They all began talking at once.

Principal Hernandez was down on his knees, shaking Sid gently, trying to wake him. "He's breathing. Can anyone call 911?" he demanded. "Does anyone have cell service?"

Gretchen's mom rushed forward and wrapped

Gretchen in a hug. Tears had swollen her cheeks and Gretchen could feel her fluttering heartbeats as they hugged.

"You're okay," Mrs. Page kept repeating. "You're okay. You're okay."

Gretchen swung away from her mother and hurried over to Coach Walker, who wrapped a fresh towel over Devra's cut. "You're not in any trouble, Devra," the coach assured her. "The bleeding has almost stopped. There might be a tiny scar. . . ."

Gretchen knelt beside Devra. "I'm so sorry," she said. "Really. I'm so sorry."

Devra blinked. "Sorry?"

"For acting like such a jerk," Gretchen said. "For accusing you of everything. For blaming you for all the terrible things that happened. All the horrible things that Sid did. I'm so sorry."

Devra narrowed her eyes at Gretchen. She shook her head. "I can't believe you're apologizing. You just saved my life!"

Gretchen stared at her, her mind spinning. "Hey, I *did*—didn't I?"

Despite the horror, both girls broke out laughing.

"A surprise party?" Gretchen said into the phone. "When?" She listened to Courtney's answer. "Ana is having a Sweet 17 party?"

"She was away for her sixteenth," Courtney explained.

"She says she was cheated. So she's doing it this year. Only she doesn't know it. We're going to throw a surprise party for her."

"Awesome," Gretchen said. "Can't wait. How are you going to surprise her?"

Before Courtney could answer, Mrs. Page entered Gretchen's room. "Who are you talking to?" she demanded.

"Got to go," Gretchen told Courtney. "My mom is here." She clicked off the call. "That was Courtney," she told her mother.

Mrs. Page couldn't hide her relief. "Nice. Sorry to interrupt." She squinted hard at Gretchen. "You feel okay? No problems from . . . from what happened?"

Gretchen raised her fist and squeezed it. "My hand still hurts from punching Sid."

"Otherwise you're okay?" her mother demanded. "I talked to Dr. Knoller. She said you seemed fine when she talked with you this morning. But she said it would be understandable if you felt a little in shock, or if you felt emotional or stressed about what you went through."

Gretchen sighed. "Please, Mom. Give it a rest. I'm okay. Really. Physically and mentally. Please believe me."

"You don't have to snap at me," Mrs. Page said. "I'm just trying to show some concern. That's all." She started to the door. "Would you like eggs for lunch?"

"That would be nice," Gretchen said. "Thanks."

She listened to her mother's footsteps going downstairs. For a long moment, she sat against the headboard of her bed, staring at the morning sunlight out the twin bedroom windows. A bright fall day. And she felt bright, too. She felt light as air, as if her problems had been solved, as if all her worries were in the past.

She heard a *ping*. From her phone. At first, she didn't recognize the sound. Then she remembered: a text message.

She picked up the phone and glanced at the screen.

And read the message:

YOU KILLED ME, GRETCHEN. BUT I'M NOT GOING AWAY. BFF. Polly